Scarred Hearts

MAX BLECHER

Translated by Henry Howard
with an introduction by Paul Bailey

First published in Romanian in 1937 as *Inimi Cicatrizate*

This translation published in 2008 by Old Street Publishing Ltd
28-32 Bowling Green Lane, London EC1R 0BJ
www.oldstreetpublishing.co.uk

ISBN 978-1-905847-18-1

Translation copyright © Old Street Publishing 2008
Introduction copyright © Paul Bailey 2008

10 9 8 7 6 5 4 3 2 1

A CIP catalogue record for this title is available from the British Library.

Printed and bound in Great Britain by J H Haynes & Co Ltd, Sparkford.

The publishers would like to thank Henry Howard for the great pains he has taken with the translation of *Scarred Hearts*. Without him this publication would not have been possible.

We would also like to thank Paul Bailey, Norman Manea and Angela Jianu for the many excellent ways in which they have supported the book.

In the last week of September 1936, the playwright and novelist Mihail Sebastian spent precious time with his friend Max (Marcel) Blecher in the town of Roman, in the north-east of Romania. Blecher had returned to the country of his birth after an eventful and traumatic year in a sanatorium in a remote region of France 'just below Boulogne' on the map. He was afflicted with a rare tubercular complaint, a form of extra-pulmonary tuberculosis that affects the spine. The exact medical term is *tuberculosis spondylitis*, but it is more commonly known as Pott's Disease, since it was first detected and treated by Percival Pott, a London surgeon, in the eighteenth century.

Max Blecher's illness was far advanced when Sebastian visited him that autumn. On his return to Bucharest, Sebastian wrote in his *Journal 1935 to 1945*, published fifty-one years after his death:

> [Blecher] is living in the intimate company of death. It is not a vague, abstract death in the long term, but his own death, precise, definite, known in detail like an object.

Sebastian continued the entry for September 30 by asking himself:

> What gives him the courage to live? What keeps him going? He is not even in despair. I swear I don't understand. How many times have I been on the verge of tears when I looked at him. At night I could hear him groaning and crying out in his room – and I felt there was someone else in the house apart

from us, a someone who was death, fate, or whatever. I came away feeling shattered, bewildered.

What gave Max Blecher the courage to live was, in part, the novel he was in the difficult process of writing. *Inimi Cicatrizate* (Scarred Hearts) would appear in February 1937 and be recognised instantly by discerning critics as the wholly remarkable work of art that it is. Blecher's elegant style inspired comparisons with Kafka and Rainer Maria Rilke, and such praise must have pleased and comforted him during the final months of his distressingly brief life (he was to die in 1938, at the age of twenty-nine). Yet the truth is that Blecher is a literary original, who found his singular authorial voice in unenviable physical and mental circumstances.

The central character in *Scarred Hearts* is a young Romanian named Emanuel, who is studying chemistry at a university in Paris. The book opens with Emanuel being subjected to a thorough medical examination, described in – for once the cliché is apt – grim detail. A wasted vertebra is located by X-ray, and then the examining doctor, gently pressing Emanuel's stomach, finds something much more worrying – a cold abscess, filled with pus leaking from the damaged bone. It is essential that the abscess is lanced, and Emanuel's regular physician, Dr Bertrand, is instructed to perform what appears to be a simple operation.

The opening chapter might lead one to expect that the rest of the novel will be in the nature of a case history. It is no such commonplace thing. *Scarred Hearts* is, as its title suggests, concerned with a number of variously unhappy people, the physically healthy as well as the chronically sick. Early on, Emanuel indicates that the narrative will involve the complex feelings of others:

> Now, as he stared at the sprawling rows of patients, his illness
> was no longer a simple matter of an abstract phrase, 'being ill' as
> opposed to 'being healthy'. He felt as if he had joined the ranks
> of a military hierarchy. He was part of the fellowship of illness,
> the fellowship of the plaster cast . . .

That fellowship, under the benign guidance of Dr Cériez, the director of the sanatorium, includes Roger Torn and Cora, devoted lovers though confined to their stretcher beds, and the aristocratic Isa, of Mongolian appearance, who comes to the clinic with her own maidservant, the endlessly attentive Celina. There is also Zed, a motorcyclist injured in an accident that has destroyed his legs, and the resourceful Ernest, who befriends Emanuel in important ways before going back to the real world. It is Ernest who ensures that Solange, with whom Emanuel is besotted, will visit the new patient, encased in his plaster corset. Solange has been cured and now functions in the real world where people are free to do as they choose and make money, but she is sympathetic to Emanuel's plight. She soon becomes his lover.

Perhaps the most memorable of these prisoners of malign fate is the seemingly resilient Quitonce, who has two sticks and walks by flinging his legs around. Quitonce, the 'son of a renowned engineer in Paris', is relatively young despite his greying hair. 'He seemed never to give a thought to his infirmity. But he confessed otherwise':

> I've been sick since I was a boy. I know all the doctors,
> all the nurses, all the sanatoriums of Europe . . . There

are international crooks who have scoured the entire globe and know precisely what city, what company is ripe for a hit . . . Well I know by heart the geography of bone disease clinics. I can tell you what sanatorium in Switzerland boasts the friendliest nurses and where in Germany you can get the best plaster . . . I am a specialist . . . In my career as a patient I have surpassed dilettantism. I have become a true professional.

Those 'friendliest nurses' are captured in some photographs, with Quitonce himself in the centre of the frame, which he shows to the frustrated Emanuel. The erotic images are resonant in the story later, when Quitonce's erstwhile virility is viewed from a saddening perspective. One by one, the patients, the members of a fellowship few would wish to join, leave Emanuel to his own deserts. There are comic interludes – a drunken party, in particular – and there are moments when Emanuel's behaviour towards the solicitous Solange is believably cold and unpleasant to the point of callous cruelty. Entombed in plaster, his putrefying flesh smarting and itching, Emanuel is decidedly not a plaster saint.

Scarred Hearts was first published eight days before my own birth in 1937, and here I am – seventy-one years later – welcoming its belated appearance in English. It is an honour to do so. Here is a work of fiction of the utmost integrity, with no easy recourse to sentimentality, which Blecher abhorred. Yet Mihail Sebastian, making his Journal entry for December 30 1936, saw a more vulnerable side to his dying friend:

As for Blecher, he is much more downcast. He spoke to me of his death, which he thinks is close at hand.

'I'm not scared of death. Then I'll rest and sleep. Ah, how well I'll stretch out, how well I'll sleep! Listen, I've begun to write a novel. But I don't feel that I absolutely must complete it [. . .] Recently I've thought of taking my own life. But it's difficult. I don't have the means. The simplest would be to hang myself – but I'd still have to bang a nail in the wall, and then Olimpia would come and I wouldn't be able to take it any further. I asked her to buy me some caustic soda on some pretext or other – but my parents didn't allow her to. How stupid I was not to buy a revolver when I could still walk and buy myself one.'

The following day, he apologised to Sebastian for his uncharacteristic confession:

Please forgive me. I don't know what came over me. I have a horror of sentimentality.

That horror is reflected in this scrupulously attentive novel, which – despite his melodramatic outburst to Sebastian – he had a compulsion to complete. Writing it kept suicidal thoughts at bay, however fleetingly. If the tone is very often melancholic, then it's an exuberant melancholy, because Emanuel's intelligence is always alert and active. *Scarred Hearts* is a masterpiece, and all the more poignant for being so beadily accurate about human behaviour in extremis. It is a book to live with, to read again and again, as only great literature demands us to.

Paul Bailey, 2008

Quel terrible souvenir à affronter.

Kierkegaard

1

EMANUEL CLIMBED THE dark staircase. The air smelt faintly of pharmaceutical products and burnt rubber. At the end of the narrow corridor he recognised the white door to which he had been directed. He entered without knocking.

The room in which he found himself appeared even older and mustier than the corridor. It was lit by a single window that diffused a bluish, uncertain light over the clutter in the little waiting room, in which periodicals lay scattered everywhere, covering the marble table and the chairs that were solemnly draped in white gowns and ready for removal, as if they had put on comfortable clothes for travelling.

Emanuel did not so much sit on as fall into one of the armchairs. He was startled to notice shadows crossing the room and suddenly realised that the window at the back was actually an aquarium where black fish swam slowly, swollen and goggle-eyed. He sat staring for a few seconds, following their lazy, gliding courses, nearly forgetting why he had come.

Why, in fact, had he come here? Ah yes! He remembered and cleared his throat so as to register his presence, but no one answered.

His temples still throbbed, but much more as a result of running all the way from Dr Bertrand's surgery than from any real anxiety. And in this sombre old room, he began to feel a little calmer.

A door opened and a woman crossed the waiting room with quick steps, disappearing through the door to the corridor. Emanuel regretted not asking her to announce that he was there.

The fish continued to drift along sadly in the gloomy light. The waiting room was so quiet and dark, so calm, that if he had been compelled to wait there for eternity, Emanuel would have had no objection. On the contrary, he would have cheerfully accepted the situation, remaining as long as possible on this side of the brutal truth which he might have to hear in a few minutes.

Behind one of the doors someone cleared their throat, a belated echo of Emanuel's own cough.

A small shadowy figure materialised in the doorway like a startled animal emerging from its lair.

'Have you been sent by Dr Bertrand? Good. I know all about you, he telephoned me… Acute pain in the lower back, isn't it? A spinal X-ray.'

The creature rubbed his hands nervously as if to get rid of the last bits of dirt that were left on his fingers from digging his lair.

His little mole eyes glittered gold and swollen in the dim light.

'We'll take a look at it right away… This way, please.'

Emanuel followed him along the corridor and found himself entering a room in complete darkness. It was from here that the heavy smell of burnt rubber originated.

A light bulb flickered feebly on. The room was cluttered with medical equipment, nickel-plated constructions made of tubes and circus crossbars.

There were so many electrical wires everywhere that Emanuel stood doubtfully in the doorway, for fear that entering and brushing against one of them would unleash a formidable discharge of thunder and sparks.

'Come in! Come in…' said the doctor, virtually taking Emanuel by the hand. 'You can undress here…'

The doctor indicated a trunk held together by screws, an enigmatic apparatus that apparently served from time to time as a couch. It was the first time in his life that Emanuel had undertaken an act as simple and intimate as undressing in such solemn surroundings.

The doctor smoked all the while, carelessly dropping the ashes onto the floor of this terrifying scientific chamber, where each square centimetre seemed charged with mystery and electricity.

'You only need take off your shirt…'

Emanuel was ready. He began to shiver.

'Are you cold?' asked the doctor. 'The whole thing only takes a minute.'

The cold, sharp contact with the tin surface on which he lay down sent an even more intense shudder through Emanuel.

'Now, pay attention… When I tell you, you need to stop breathing… I'd like to get a good X-ray.'

The doctor opened and closed the metal box. The light went out. The release mechanism fell open with a clang. A handle dropped cleanly, cutting a straight line in the darkness. The current set up a muffled vibration, like the growling of an irritated animal. The whole procedure was metallic and precise, like that game of concentration in which a nickel-plated ball is guided meticulously from one groove to the next.

'Now!'

Emanuel held his breath. The pounding of heart seemed to resonate through the tin table on which he lay. The darkness buzzed in his ears.

Then came a new noise, a hissing that grew in intensity, then abruptly ceased, like a hot coal dropped in water.

'You can breathe,' came the doctor's voice again.

The light came on. Emanuel experienced a moment of sudden, extreme lucidity. What was he doing there, stretched out upon that table? What for?

He had an absolute conviction that he was gravely ill. The evidence was plain from everything around him. What was the significance of all these machines? They were clearly not made for the healthy.

And in the very instant that he found himself there, in the midst of them, cornered by them…

The doctor extracted the plate from the metal table.

'Please don't put your clothes on yet. I need to see if it came out well. Just stay there… lying down.'

The doctor picked up Emanuel's jacket and placed it over his chest, covering him with tender care; only his mother had ever done that, when he was a child, wrapping him in his blanket before he went to sleep.

What would the doctor say? What would the plate show? That ghastly plate...

He felt well once more under the soft, warm coat. If it hadn't been for the sharp, unpleasant chill of the tin beneath him and the want of something other than a metal crossbar to rest his head on, he might have fallen asleep. He shivered slightly from the cold, but otherwise he felt overwhelmed by a pleasant, restful fatigue.

A door slammed somewhere at the end of the corridor. Life was going on then, in the distance... As he was, he felt withdrawn from it, there beneath the shelter of his coat, naked on the X-ray table.

'The X-ray has come out well,' the doctor said as he emerged from his office. 'But it looks like one of your vertebrae has been badly attacked... There is a piece of bone missing from it...'

The doctor said all this in rapid French that Emanuel could not really understand, and also with an interruption when he burned his fingers on the cigarette butt which he had picked up from the table and inhaled greedily.

Emanuel was confused, not fully understanding him. There was a piece of bone missing from his vertebra? But how could it have disappeared? He asked the doctor this.

'It has been eaten away... eaten away by microbes,' replied the dark little man. 'All wasted away... like a decayed tooth.'

'Actually in the spine?'

'Yes, actually in the spine… a wasted vertebra…'

Then why hasn't my body collapsed yet, Emanuel thought, since the very axis of its support is broken? He remembered that he needed to put his clothes back on, but dared move only with infinite care and attention, constantly supporting himself on the medical apparatus. His chest had become a chasm in which he could hear a loud noise like the roaring in a seashell when you put it next to your ear. The thumping of his heart resounded in the emptiness. It would be possible, he realised, for his body to disintegrate between one moment and the next, like a felled tree, like a rag doll.

Once, at the pension where he lived, he had set a mousetrap on the floor in his room and a mouse had become caught in it in the middle of the night. Emanuel turned on the light and saw it running round and round, maddened by fright in the trap's wire mesh. By sunrise the mouse was no longer there; it had managed to open the tiny gate and make its escape. But now it was staggering about the room in such confusion and terror, and moving so slowly and uncertainly that he would have been able to catch it in his hand. Several times the mouse went past the entrance to its own mouse-hole and sniffed it a little, but it had not gone inside… It was completely disorientated by trauma and fatigue from the night spent in the trap.

As he returned to the dressing-trunk with his things, Emanuel was so cautious and weak in his movements that he reminded himself of the mouse creeping about on the floor. He was not so much walking as dragging himself along. He identified with that mouse down to the smallest detail. So totally terrified, so totally bewildered were his movements…

The doctor went back into his office. Emanuel thought suddenly of suicide, of hanging himself with his belt from one of the metal bars. But this thought was so weak and ineffective that it didn't even have sufficient power to make him lift a hand. It was certainly a fine idea, just as fine as, for example, the mouse returning to its hole, but equally vague and unrealistic.

In any case, he wasn't alone for long. The doctor returned, holding the still-wet negative for him to see. He switched on a brighter light bulb and placed the X-ray in its light. Emanuel stared, mystified and distracted, at the black shadows representing the skeleton; the most intimate, secret structure of his body was printed there in dark, funereal transparence.

'Look. Here… this is a healthy vertebra,' explained the doctor. 'And here, further down, that's the one missing a piece of bone… you can see clearly where it's eroded.'

One vertebra was indeed shorter than the rest.

'It's called Pott's Disease… spinal tuberculosis.'

Everything seemed entirely clear now that this erosion had its own scientific name.

'There is something else that concerns me here…' the doctor continued, and pointed to a large, funnel-like shadow. 'I am afraid it might be an abscess… I'll need to examine you in my office.'

Up to this point the doctor had spoken uninterruptedly, without looking at his patient. When he lifted his eyes and saw Emanuel's face, ashen and petrified, he hurried into the office to put away the X-ray, then came back, grasped Emanuel's hands, and began to shake him.

'Hey, come on! What's this? Courage... a little courage! It's curable... you will go to Berck... That's your solution... a little courage. A little courage!'

He pulled him along after him the whole length of the corridor and through the waiting room where, shut behind glass, the fish went on unconcernedly with their hermetic migration.

They went into the doctor's examination room. Here too the curtains were drawn, here too it was dark, here too a single bulb was burning amidst a petrified torrent of books and medicines. The little man made his way nimbly between them; he almost seemed to brush them in passing and sniff them out with an animal's sense of smell.

'Let's see your back first.' Emanuel lay face-down on a couch covered with a white sheet. The doctor began running his fingers, slowly and carefully up and down his spine, palpating each vertebra like a piano tuner testing an instrument's keys. When the doctor pressed hard on one of them, a stabbing pain sang out. 'It's exactly what the X-ray shows... this is the diseased vertebra.' The doctor applied more force and in his spine the same clear note of agony sang out once more.

'I don't mean to pry, but why did you come to France?' the doctor asked while examining him. 'I gather from your accent that you're a foreigner.'

'Yes,' replied Emanuel. 'I came here for my studies.'

'And what is your field?' the doctor asked.

'Chemistry.'

'Ah! Chemistry... do you like chemistry? Is it something that interests you?'

I am only interested in life now, Emanuel wanted to reply, but he said nothing.

'Do you think your parents will be able to support you here, in a place by the sea? You will need a great deal of rest, good nutrition… above all, peace and quiet… at Berck for instance, by the seaside, in a sanatorium there…'

'I will write to my father in Romania,' replied Emanuel. 'I think he will help me.'

Curiously, the word that the doctor had spoken, 'sanatorium' suddenly brought a pleasant, sunny memory to Emanuel's mind, a cool breeze in the suffocating atmosphere of the medical examination room. The previous year, when he had spent a month at Tekirghiol in order to cure his supposed rheumatism (this being the diagnosis every previous doctor had given for his back pain), he had become obsessed with the idea that he would be living in a sanatorium very soon. He perfectly recalled a sunny morning on the beach, his friends playing cards in the shadow of a parasol, stretched out on their bellies in the sand, where the sudden, irrational urge had crossed his mind to say his farewells, to say that he was leaving for a sanatorium.

Now, in the gloomy office, in the single bulb's anaemic light, this memory was a breath of bright, fresh air amongst the dusty papers.

'And now let's look at your stomach.'

Emanuel rolled over. The doctor put out his palm and was running it lightly over his skin when he stopped short, staring with amazement into Emanuel's eyes.

'How long have you had this?'

He pointed to a thick round swelling on his abdomen, smooth and well-defined like an egg, that had grown beneath the skin near his hip. (It's enormous, thought Emanuel, thoroughly frightened). He tried in vain to remember; he had never seen it before. Not even Dr Bertrand had noticed it. Perhaps it was something new that had appeared during the last few hours.

'In any case, it's a good thing we discovered it in time,' said the doctor. 'If that bursts, it will be a fine spectacle… it's a cold abscess full of pus draining from the diseased bone… it'll need to be lanced… the pus will need to be extracted with a syringe.'

So many horrific things had occurred, so sententiously and so calmly, during the last hour; so much catastrophe had taken place, that, exhausted as he was by the day's excitement, for a delirious, irrational moment Emanuel felt like laughing.

Dr Bertrand's examination, the X-ray, the eroded vertebra and now the cold abscess; it all seemed preordained. He was expecting the doctor to open the door any second and ask him into the next room, *Come in please, the guillotine awaits you…*

But the doctor was silent, his eyes fixed on the abscess.

'What needs to happen now?' Emanuel asked weakly, his voice coming from another world.

'The puncture, of course!' replied the doctor. 'First of all, the puncture. My advice is to get it done by Dr Bertrand, who sent you to me for X-raying. I can telephone him if you like. He has a very steady hand. Anyway we're not talking about a difficult operation… a simple puncture with the needle… that's all. I will tell him to bring whatever is necessary. What is your address?'

While the doctor wrote down the address in his notebook,

Emanuel took a few deep breaths to free himself from a sense of oppression. He listened anxiously to what the doctor was saying.

'... Then, after a few days, you will go to Berck-sur-Mer...'

'Berck?' asked Emanuel. 'Where exactly is that?'

The doctor took down an enormous *Larousse* from the shelf and opened it at the map of France.

'Here it is... you see?... the English Channel... that's Berck, just below Boulogne... it's not on the map. It's a little beach, lost among the dunes, a little sea town where patients like yourself come from all over the world to take the cure. They spend their time lying on their backs, in body casts, but they lead absolutely normal lives. They even go out in carriages, you know, special carriages drawn by horses or donkeys, in which they can lie flat on their backs.'

The doctor muttered this whole explanation in an erudite tone, staring at the book as if he was reading out everything he said from the dictionary.

'But what if the swelling bursts on my way home?' asked Emanuel.

He would have liked to ask far more questions: wouldn't his spine shatter on his way to the pension, wouldn't he collapse on the street, wouldn't his head tumble from his shoulders and go rolling along the pavement like a bowling ball? Within the last few minutes, he had begun to feel how very tenuously he was held together. Workers in glass factories amuse themselves by pitching globs of melted glass into water – the pieces become harder and more resistant than regular glass, enough to withstand a hammer blow, but should so much as a tiny splinter break off, the whole mass turns to powder. Wouldn't a single splintered vertebra be enough, possibly, to transform his whole body into dust? While he was walking down the street the diseased bone might come away, and Emanuel would crumble on the spot, with nothing left of him but a heap of smoking ash.

The doctor calmed him with scientific and medical arguments.

As for the fee, he wouldn't accept anything. 'I don't take money from students...' he said, his tiny, glittering eyes burning. Emanuel felt so overcome by a rush of tender affection that his own eyes welled with tears. He thanked the doctor with exaggerated effusiveness. He luxuriated ecstatically in his appreciation, like a prisoner tasting freedom. He thought of throwing himself at the doctor's feet and lying prostrate before him.

'Thank you, Doctor. Thank you!' (Hosanna! Hosanna!)

He hurriedly dressed and made his way out through the waiting room.

'Courage!' said the doctor once more on the stairs, with a little click of his tongue like an animal tamer goading on his charge to jump through a hoop.

'Courage! Courage!' The words resounded within Emanuel, re-echoing off the walls of his chest.

Suddenly he was standing out in the open street, out in the open daylight. It was like a sudden, immense expansion of the world. Houses still existed, then, and real asphalt, and a distant sky, indistinct and white. He had left the outside world in this light, and now he found it again, the same as before, even more vast and empty maybe, even more filled with clear air, even less cluttered compared with the dark rooms of the doctor's surgery.

Yet everything seemed much sadder, more indifferent… A blighted Emanuel walked this world, a man with an eroded vertebra, an unfortunate before whom the houses parted in fear. He stepped softly on the pavement, as if floating on the asphalt. In the interval spent shut inside the doctor's office, the world had become strangely diluted. The boundaries of objects still existed, but merely as thin lines that, like in a drawing, surround a house in order to make it a house or stabilise the outline of a man; those contours that enclose things and people, trees and dogs, while barely possessing the strength to hold within their limits so much matter on the verge of collapse. It would be enough for someone to loosen that thin line around the edges of things for those imposing houses, their own outline suddenly wanting, to dissolve into a murky, homogenous grey sludge.

He, Emanuel himself, was no more than a mass of meat and bones, sustained only by the rigidity of a profile.

He was surprised by the thought that he hadn't eaten anything all day. What was that thought doing there at such a moment? Emanuel realised bitterly that even in such an imprecise and uncertain world he would still have to perform the same definite actions as before.

He headed for a restaurant. He used to take a table in a small, studenty establishment in the old quarter of the city. Office workers and labourers would go there too; you ate badly and quickly there, and it was always crowded with customers standing waiting for the next table and still-warm seat.

This was the first time he had come very late, when there was nobody there. The restaurant was empty, silent and thick with smoke. The waitresses were eating at a corner table. The cashier ate at her desk, behind a wooden frame, as if fated to perform all the functions of her existence there, perched on her chair, a captive in a rigid coop. There was an overwhelming silence in the restaurant, like the aftermath of a cataclysm. Chairs were scattered all about the room and Emanuel could find only a single table still covered with its cloth. All the others had been stripped bare.

He sat down carefully, fearful of disturbing his abscess.

Around him, the walls were covered in large mirrors framed in bronze that reflected the same empty room from one to the other, each one more faded and greenish than the last, until, far away in the farthest of reflections, the room had become as aqueous as the fish-tank in the doctor's waiting-room.

There, far off amidst the murky, stagnant water, floated solitary and pallid the bloated carp-like face of the cashier, gazing sluggishly out of her round, cold eye.

She was the only ocean creature in that submarine abyss, and Emanuel the lone drowned sailor.

2

THE CONCIERGE WAS waiting impatiently at the entrance to the pension. She spotted him from a distance and waved.

'Dr Bertrand's surgery called. He's coming at four, bringing everything necessary with him. That's what they said – and also that you should be in bed.'

'Understood,' replied Emanuel, anxious to get indoors. But the concierge, consumed with curiosity and impatience, stopped him in the doorway.

'What's wrong with you? Why are you so pale? Are you ill? Is it something serious?'

She grabbed his jacket and began to shake him like a sack she wanted to empty of its contents.

'Not so fast! Not so fast!' Emanuel calmed her down. 'Let's go to my room and I'll tell you.'

His room was small and fairly uncomfortable, situated on the ground floor next to the concierge's own. He had chosen it so as not to have to climb any stairs with his sore back.

He began to undress. How many times would he have to undress that day? He recalled an Englishman who had committed suicide, leaving a note that read 'All this buttoning and unbuttoning'. Now, for the third time that day, he stretched out on a bed, while the concierge continued to rankle him with her questions. Then Colette came into the room.

Colette lived in the same pension. She was a straightforward girl, as easy to read as a sheet of paper. She worked as an embroiderer and seamstress, doing small alteration jobs in her room. She and Emanuel would make antiseptic love together, without any great sense of pleasure. Afterwards Colette would make him hot tea flavoured with vanilla. Tea and vanilla epitomised the whole scent and savour of their domesticated, well-mannered lovemaking.

The concierge began to tidy up the room and Colette straightened the books on the table so that Dr Bertrand would find everything neatly arranged. Meanwhile Emanuel wrote a telegram to his father in Romania.

Colette couldn't make a proper, conventional display of the sorrow which had overtaken her. She wanted simply to burst into tears but, knowing this would upset Emanuel, she restrained herself. She hurried to take the telegram to the post-office, glad to escape for a moment that room in which her heart felt heavy with tears. The concierge left the room with her.

Emanuel found himself suddenly alone, lying in bed, at a time of the afternoon when normally he would be at work at the university.

He was overwhelmed by a serene, agreeable feeling of laziness, like an old echo of childhood, reminding him of the times he was 'ill' and lay in bed instead of going to school. He gingerly touched the swelling on his hip and shuddered. It seemed to be still growing. Terrified, he lay motionless among the pillows, face up, barely breathing.

This was how Dr Bertrand found him.

'Well, aren't you full of surprises? What's happened? I heard horrible things on the phone...' the doctor said as he came in. He spoke with the dignified joviality common to family doctors who, on attaining a certain age, all acquire the same tone of voice, as if it were a common biological characteristic of their professional development. He was tall and broad-shouldered, his close-cropped hair standing on end like bristles on a brush.

He examined the abscess with an impassive face on which Emanuel could read nothing of his inner thoughts.

Someone knocked on the door. The doctor's assistant came in, loaded down with bags of instruments and various nickel-plated boxes.

'Yes... it's exactly what I was told on the phone. The abscess must be punctured right away,' the doctor said calmly. 'Let's get going!'

He took off his jacket and rolled up his sleeves. Then he asked for water to wash his hands. The concierge hurried in and bustled around anxiously, thrilled to be of even the smallest service to such an eminent personage as Dr Bertrand. The assistant set out the nickel boxes on the table. When everything was ready, he pulled the bed into the light of the window.

Emanuel removed his shirt. His teeth began to chatter once more, as they had done in the X-ray room. He tried unsuccessfully to interpret from the assistant's movements, to spot some instrument of torture, to make out the size of the needle. The doctor and his assistant busied themselves with the various objects on the table; Emanuel was aware of nothing save their metallic tinkling.

Outside, in the street beyond the curtain, a man walked by hurriedly. With his ears Emanuel followed the distinct steps on the asphalt. What worries did that man have? There he was, walking unconcernedly down the street, while Emanuel himself lay on the bed, about to endure a terrible puncturing... Now he was genuinely quaking with fear.

The doctor turned toward the bed holding a wad of cotton soaked in iodine. He wore large red rubber gloves, like a lorry driver.

He swabbed the swelling and half of the surface of Emanuel's stomach, which quickly turned yellow. An antiseptic, clinical smell of iodoform permeated the bedroom; it gave the room a new reality, medical and extremely severe. Something serious and inevitable was taking place. Emanuel felt completely bewildered. Around him he saw his wardrobe, the books and the table, the old familiar things, the well-known things, but now they came unstuck, indecipherable in their murky lucidity, like the chaotic words shouted by an unknown voice in a throng of people crowding out an assembly hall.

'Anaesthetic,' said the doctor laconically.

The only thing Emanuel could see was the assistant approaching the bed with a large glass tube. The doctor covered Emanuel's face with his shirt and told the concierge to take hold of his hands. The big test-tube gave a sudden hiss and Emanuel felt, in a place just above the abscess, an ice-cold gush of liquid on his skin that stiffened the flesh around it.

A metallic box opened and closed.

'Needle,' said the doctor, as the assistant approached once more.

'The needle… now he's going to stab me with the needle…' thought Emanuel. Each second throbbed terribly in his temples.

Now?

He felt a heavy jab next to his hip, like someone punching him with all their might. It was a dull, undefined pain that weighed horribly on the pelvis. A claw digging into flesh frozen by the anaesthetic, a torture both detached and extremely present.

He opened his eyes a crack and through part of the shirt he spied the assistant pumping something into a bottle; he couldn't make out anything else. What was taking place down there in his flesh? What was the doctor doing?

A deeper thrust of the needle wrenched a groan of pain out of him. How much longer would it last? It seemed endless, and the assistant was still pumping…

Finally there was a pause… Emanuel felt the needle suddenly withdrawn from his flesh, and began to breathe more easily. The muscles next to the swelling remained horribly stiff, but the pain was more straightforward now, stabilised at a constant level of intensity.

The concierge lifted the shirt off his eyes. The doctor was swabbing ether onto a little spot that bled a little. The bottle on the table was full of thick yellowish liquid.

'What's that?' Emanuel asked, worn out by the strain and agitation.

'Pus, my friend! Pus!' replied the doctor with his usual joviality. 'You need to go to Berck and rest quietly there till you're cured. It's a matter requiring plenty of time and patience. Your abscess was filled to the brim. I doubt it will build up again that quickly… Stay resting. Do you hear? You must be good and stay lying on your back… When are you going?'

'In a few days,' Emanuel replied, exhausted. 'I telegraphed my father and I'm expecting him at the end of the week. He'll come on the first train, I'm sure.'

He wanted to ask more questions, but was browbeaten by the doctor's impassive face. He became irritated then by the thought that behind that indifference lay a perfect knowledge of his illness. The doctor gripped his hand and left.

In his room the afternoon resumed its idle, disconsolate course. The bottle of pus stood in full view on the table. A few copper-coloured sunbeams played in the soft light on the wall of the house opposite. Emanuel felt a great weariness in his chest – as if he were breathing in something of the barren and desolate content of that melancholy afternoon.

He tried to read, but couldn't understand a thing; books were written for another light; no book in the world could fill the immense void of this one warm day of intimate tedium and suffering. This is the ineluctable misery of illness.

Across the street the sunset's rays climbed the ashen grey wall, up to the rooftops where they set the garret windows alight with purple flames. The house's unmoving, abandoned appearance rent his heart.

Very slowly he lifted his blanket to look at the place where the swelling had been; he felt no pain, and the swelling was gone. He examined his naked legs, his stomach, his thighs, his whole body...

Colette caught him unawares as he was counting his ribs.

The days passed, arid and colourless, fearfully long and miserable. Colette would sit beside him, embroidering. A few colleagues came to see him on their way home from the university, which was nearby. They came in reeking of laboratory acid, which only added to his misery. He felt more acutely than ever that he was ill, that he was off work...

He would lie motionless for hours on end, his head raised slightly on the pillows.

'I am doing my apprenticeship in illness,' he would tell Colette.

Each day around four o'clock he pricked up his ears at the sound of the concierge's footsteps when she delivered the mail. But the usual disappointment followed. No telegram, no letter? 'Nothing.' The day would descend again into monotony.

One evening after dinner, while Emanuel was absently flicking through a newspaper in his bed by the window, he sensed that someone had stopped in the street and was staring attentively at him. The concierge had forgotten to close the shutters. He pushed the curtain aside slightly. On the pavement, looking back at him, was his father.

Emanuel was all excited; his father hid his own disquiet as he walked into the room, clearing his throat to stop his voice trembling. He loved Emanuel with an intensity that sometimes disturbed his son. Emanuel felt himself morally indebted to his father's love, and, if only for that reason, he was sincerely sorry that he had become ill. During the last few days he had thought with terror, with dread, of what might happen if he should die. 'My father would surely go mad with grief,' he told himself, imagining the calm, disciplined dementia of this man who did everything in life with cold-blooded imperturbability. 'For a man like him, madness would have to be incredibly well organised,' Emanuel thought with infinite sorrow. This too was a particular kind of self-indulgence.

In an instant the room's atmosphere changed. His father took his illness in hand like a tangled business affair that needed sorting out without delay. He resolved to go first by himself to Berck for the day, to talk to the doctors there and look for a suitable sanatorium. He left the very next day and returned late that night. He was full of enthusiasm about Berck.

'That's where your cure lies. The patients lead normal lives in sanatoria set up like normal hotels; you won't even think of yourself as being ill. You'll see… you'll see…'

The next morning they packed Emanuel's things and in the afternoon they were ready to go.

At the last moment, the concierge discreetly slipped Emanuel a package she had brought.

'It's from Mlle Colette…' she whispered.

Out of curiosity more than anything else, Emanuel opened it straight away. It contained a box of tea and a few cubes of meat extract for making soup.

The tea was clearly an allusion to their love.

As for the cubes, Colette had racked her brains all morning to think of an inexpensive and useful gift and in the end had recalled that, during the war, her mother had sent meat extract to her father (who was fighting at the front) so that he could make soup for himself in the trenches.

'And where he is going, it must be worse than in the trenches…' she thought innocently. 'A warm plate of soup will do him good…'

And with this thought her eyes welled with tears.

3

THE DAY LENGTHENED into an October twilight, lukewarm and funereal. Fields paraded before the train window, red and copper and putrid from the sun in which they had been bathed all summer long. Alone in the compartment, Emanuel and his father lay submerged in a shared feeling of tacit intimacy. They trundled along with the rhythm of the train's old ironwork, like the rapid beating of an ageing mechanical heart set beneath the carriage.

They got out at a little station where the train stopped for less than a minute.

They boarded another, smaller, train with narrow carriages and an old-fashioned engine, humped like a camel. There were just two benches in their carriage, set along the whole length on either side, like the ones in a tram.

Slowly and uncertainly the train set off, jerking and jolting on the tracks. All the windows started chattering their teeth noisily, as if they were scared of the journey. Emanuel gazed behind him one last time at the little white train station with pink climbing roses over its windows. Then someone drew a curtain and the landscape was left outside as if cut off with scissors.

Inside the carriage was a great crowd of people with bags and baskets; men crammed onto the benches… children whimpering… Then, as the train gathered speed, noisy conversation began to fill the whole carriage, settling into a general buzz of goodwill and understanding.

Everyone was on their way to Berck. A farmer in his Sunday clothes and clutching a bouquet of wildflowers gesticulated exaggeratedly about his son's illness to a thin lady in an elegant grey suit.

On the bench opposite, two young parents were taking their child to a sanatorium. He was a thin, pale boy in a sailor suit, with one leg shrouded in bandages. His arms dangled scrawny and lifeless, like a rag doll's. Held fast in his mother's arms, the child's gaze of deep perplexity wandered over the carriage, curiously examining this whole unfamiliar world.

Emanuel was suddenly addressed by the person sitting next to him, a little old lady in widow's black:

'Are you going to Berck?' she asked. 'Are you ill?'

She was shouting at the top of her voice in order to be heard above the combined noise of the train and the general conversation.

'Where does it hurt? Here…? Here…?'

She pointed to his hip, then to his back.

'Yes, here, in my back,' Emanuel replied.

The little old lady pursed her lips and shook her head compassionately.

'And do you have an abscess?' she went on.

There was no mistake, Emanuel had heard her correctly: she was talking about an abscess. How could this woman know what an abscess was? His face betrayed such bewilderment that the old lady made haste to soothe him.

'You see, I know a little about medicine too… I've been coming to Berck so long that I've had time to learn all about it… I have a son who is a patient there too.'

Emanuel didn't answer, and realised his sleeve was being tugged.

'I asked you something,' the old lady continued irritably. 'Do you or do you not have an abscess?'

'Yes, I do,' Emanuel replied with a certain brusqueness. 'What's it to you?'

This time the old lady said nothing. In the calligraphy of wrinkles on her face there was a clear sign of some great sadness. In a half-voice she ventured to ask if the abscess had been fistulised.

'What does "fistulised" mean?' asked Emanuel, puzzled.

'I mean, has it been lanced…? Is there a hole that allows it to drain continuously…?'

'No,' replied Emanuel. 'So far the doctor has drained the pus with a needle but now I can see the swelling is coming back.'

The train's antiquated ironwork never stopped rattling, and its noise quietly underpinned the conversation like the background murmur of an opera chorus while the soloist is singing. They were now going through the dunes that surrounded the town. In a few minutes more they would reach Berck. The entire journey had taken little more than a quarter of an hour.

'It's a good thing the abscess is not fistulised,' muttered the old lady.

'And if it were?' replied Emanuel absently.

'Ah well, then it's another matter…' And leaning into his ear, she whispered breathlessly: 'The word at Berck is that an open abscess is an open gateway to death.'

'What's she saying?' asked his father.

'You suppose I can understand her? She speaks too fast…'

The brakes of the little, worn-out train began to squeal to a stop. They had arrived. The station looked just like any other provincial railway halt. A tall man on crutches was waiting for the lady in the grey suit. Other than that there was no one on the platform. The great surprise, however, awaited Emanuel once he had made his way out.

While the driver loaded the suitcases into a car, Emanuel stood for a few moments in the little square in front of the station, looking around. He suddenly gave a start.

What on earth was it? A mobile coffin, a stretcher? A man lay on a narrow wooden bed, a sort of mattress on a frame, mounted on a base with four big rubber-tyred wheels. The man, however, was dressed normally from head to toe. He wore a tie, a beret on his head, a jacket, and yet he was motionless, neither standing nor walking around like everyone else. From his supine position he bought a newspaper from a vendor, paid for it and opened it up to read it with his head propped up on pillows, while behind him a man began to push the stretcher through the streets of the town.

'You see,' his father told him, 'all the patients here lead normal lives... They dress normally, they go about on the streets... only they do it all lying down... that's all... You'll see others as well, lying down and driving their carriages on their own...'

Emanuel was too amazed to know precisely what he thought. In the car he spent the whole time staring out of the window in the hope of spotting a patient in a carriage, but there was none to be seen. At a crossroads, looking between two rows of tall houses, he caught a sudden distant glimpse of a glittering azure streak of ocean, lying on the sand like a sword in flames.

The director was waiting for them on the doorstep of the sanatorium. The entrance was graced with two large exotic plants. The faience vases, along with the director's solemn black suit and white spats, added a decidedly theatrical note to their arrival. The director bowed and shook the father's hand first, then Emanuel's. He had a heavily powdered face, and had only just thrown away the butt of the cigar he had been smoking. With a cigar in the corner of his mouth, he acquired long bulldog wrinkles on his face, reminding Emanuel of those porcelain dogs dressed in red tailcoats that are used as ornamental ashtrays. 'Too bad the tailcoat is missing,' he thought.

The silence of the sanatorium was impressive, but the corridors were no different from corridors in hotels, with their rows of numbered white doors. Emanuel's room was on the third floor. They went slowly up in a lift that made no sound beyond a low, muffled rumble. At the far end of a dark corridor, the director opened a door. It was clear that the room was one of the cheap ones. The only furniture was a wardrobe, a table and an iron bed. In one corner was a washstand with an enormous blue enamel metal jug.

'Do you like it?' asked his father once the doctor had gone.

What was there to like? He stretched out exhausted on the bed and shut his eyes. The train's motion still buzzed in his head, along with fragments of his conversation with the little old lady in mourning. The days he had spent in bed had weakened him terribly. His father turned on the light. The room had that strange, unpleasant atmosphere associated with the sort of miserable hotel bedroom in which one sometimes has to spend the night while journeying.

Eventually someone knocked on the door.

'Eva,' the nurse introduced herself curtly as she walked in. She had a nose so long and pointed that no matter what direction she was facing, she only ever seemed to be showing her profile.

She quickly ascertained Emanuel's condition.

'You'll get well here,' she drawled in an uninterested, professional tone of voice.

'Are there many other patients with the same illness as me?' he inquired. 'Do all of them have an eroded vertebra?'

Eva threw up her arms like a supplicant from antiquity.

'One vertebra? A single vertebra? Ha! Ha! There are people here with ten eroded vertebrae… Others with a diseased knee… hip… fingers… ankle… Did you think you were the only one? Ha! Ha!'

She chuckled harshly.

Emanuel was particularly disturbed by the idea of a spine

with ten eroded vertebrae in a row; he formed a mental picture of a cigarette, forgotten in an ashtray, its whole length slowly turning to ash. 'What a wretched way to disintegrate...' he thought.

'What about Dr Cériez?' asked Emanuel's father, 'When does he come to the clinic? I spoke to him when I was here before, and...'

'Oh, very well! Very well!' interrupted Eva. 'Dr Cériez happens to be in the sanatorium now. He came to see a patient he operated on... I'll go and get him.'

Emanuel, exhausted, lay quietly on the bed. His father bustled about, the door opened and closed; there was a great deal of activity around him in which he had no part. The world seemed to have become at the same time denser yet more indistinct... The one constant thing that he could clearly feel within himself was a sense of immense exhaustion within himself. In a room somewhere in the distance, an accordion wheezed an asthmatic, mournful lament.

The nurse returned a few minutes later, accompanied by Dr Cériez.

He was still a young man, very tall and broad-shouldered, though his hair was greying. He had a superb hairstyle, a lion's mane, carefully combed back. His face was wide and stony. Only his clear blue gaze suggested otherwise, hinting at an infinite goodness, and giving to his features a mixture of childlikeness and severity.

He examined Emanuel carefully, looked over the X-rays, felt the abscess and gave the same diagnosis: spinal tuberculosis.

'Here in Berck the air is healthy and invigorating. Make sure you go for plenty of drives in the carriage, and above all stay lying down and rest yourself...'

And then, addressing the nurse: 'For the time being, leave him like this... in bed... Tomorrow, bring a stretcher-bed... Then, in a few days, once he gets used to lying down, we'll put him in a cast.'

'A cast,' murmured Emanuel apprehensively.

The doctor turned to him.

'A cast is nothing to be afraid of... Absolutely nothing to be afraid of! You'll settle into your corset as comfortably as an armchair... That I can guarantee you.'

He shook Emanuel's hand and picked up his hat, to leave. He paused for a moment.

'Do you know anyone at the sanatorium? Have you made any friends yet?'

And when Emanuel shook his head, the doctor went on:

'I will send Ernest your way. He's a fine fellow. You'll get along very well.'

He hurried out. Emanuel's father closed the door behind him slowly, with deference, as if the doctor, simply by touching the door handle, had left it imbued with some trace – some portion of his eminent personality.

'You see?' he said jovially, rubbing his hands.

As far as he was concerned the entire question of the illness was now completely resolved.

Emanuel waited for Ernest for a while, but it seemed Ernest did not intend to appear that evening. He began to undress for bed; he was neither hungry nor thirsty. A calm weariness bathed all his limbs.

As darkness fell in the room, the echo of the accordion shrouded the day's end in melancholy.

4

E MANUEL STAYED IN bed the entire morning. His father had
pulled up a chair beside him and there they remained, hand in
hand, by the untidy room's open window, staring out at the ocean's
luminous immensity. From the horizon came a milk-white blaze,
obscuring the distant outline of the dunes and the shadows of the
houses, drowning them in a blinding aureole. The hissing waves
sounded so close that nothing else could be heard from inside the
sanatorium. An electric bell rang from time to time somewhere
in the building, startling them and snatching them momentarily
from their state of bright serenity.

Eventually an attendant came to dress Emanuel. From now on
this man would come to help every day. He was extremely skilful;
he slowly pulled on the trousers, while Emanuel simply lay there;

then he put on a shirt and jacket, without haste and without forcing Emanuel to do anything but lean a little to one side or the other in order to insert his arms into the sleeves.

'He's dressing me exactly like he would a corpse,' thought Emanuel; he wanted to say as much to his father but restrained himself.

The attendant opened the door and wheeled a trolley into the room. It was the bed on which Emanuel would have to lie at all times from now on. It was fitted with a new mattress covered with black oilcloth and had two firm pillows at its head.

'Allow me,' said the attendant, and helped him slide from the bed on which he lay onto the stretcher-bed. 'From now on,' he said, 'you'll have to sleep on it, like the rest of the patients… But we can leave the iron bed in the room if you want. It's useful for putting books and things on…'

Just then a gong sounded for mealtime.

'Will you be coming down to the dining room or staying in your room?' the servant inquired.

Emanuel, in turn, asked his father with his eyes.

'Certainly. We'll go down… it's better,' he said.

The attendant pushed the trolley slowly down the corridor and into the lift.

Still intoxicated by the light and the tranquility of the morning, Emanuel treated the gentle gliding of the sprung trolley as a playful diversion. He was overcome with a light, agreeable giddiness as soon as the lift began to descend.

Only when he entered the dining room downstairs did a full understanding of his illness awaken in him. Only there, for the first time, did he have any real sense of the awfulness of the life he would have to lead from then on.

It was an ordinary restaurant dining room, vast, high, white, with curtains at the windows and large exotic plants in the corners. But who had conceived the solemn, hospitalesque arrangement of this room? What sort of director had staged this ordered, hallucinatory spectacle?

Lined up along the walls, the patients lay on their stretcher-beds, two to a table. It might have resembled a banquet from antiquity, with the guests lounging supine at their tables, if the drained, pallid faces of the worst sufferers hadn't shattered any illusions of jovial guests or cheery festivities.

What murky imagination had fashioned elements of reality into such a dolorous picture, so fantastical and so demented?

There is a sensationalist novel in which the writer imagines a perfidious and capricious queen who has mummified her lovers and arranged their coffins in a circular chamber.

How pale and colourless was that writer's vision, though, compared to the dreadful reality in this dining room filled with the living dead, encrusted in rigid poses, stretched out, mummified, and yet still throbbing with life!

Emanuel was placed at a table next to a patient in a blue dress. The strangest and most hallucinatory thing about our dreams is that the bizarrest of incidents take place in familiar and mundane surroundings. In the dining room, the elements of dream and reality were present simultaneously to such an extent that for a moment or two Emanuel felt his consciousness beginning to unravel. Everything had become extraordinarily transparent and yet dauntingly ephemeral and uncertain. What was happening? Was it actually him, Emanuel, that body lying on the trolley, in the middle of a dining-room where all the guests ate lying down at tables decorated with flower arrangements? What did it all mean? Was he living? Dreaming? In what world precisely, in what reality was all this taking place?

His table companion smiled at him in a mirror. She was lying on her carriage fully dressed and apparently normal, but her head was not propped up on pillows. She kept it lying flat, and moved it neither to the right nor the left. In order to see what was going on around her, she had a metal frame holding a mirror right above her. She could adjust this to face in any direction she wished and in this way see everything in the room. Her detached face floated in the polished crystal like a severed head in one of those cheap fairground optical illusions, and it was there that Emanuel saw the smile she was directing at him.

'Have you been ill a long time?' the girl asked without any other introduction.

'I've been suffering for many years,' replied Emanuel, 'but they hadn't found out what the illness was until now…'

'It was the same with all of us,' she replied with a slight sigh.

To his right Emanuel found a young man with his head buried in a book. He scanned the patients one by one, some completely flat on their backs, some with heads raised on pillows, others sitting up in their carriages as if in chairs, with only their legs stretched out. All were conventionally dressed, the women with a degree of coquettishness, the men in normal suits with collars and ties. They looked like an ordinary crowd of people that, at some command, had all lain down on trolleys.

He ventured to ask his table companion why certain patients lay flat on their backs, while others were only half-lying.

'They don't all have the same disease,' the young girl answered. 'Some have problems with their neck vertebrae, like me for instance. For others it's only their knees or thighs.'

She spoke with charming spontaneity and with a constant smile in the mirror. Emanuel attempted to reply with a smile of his own, but his lips found themselves set in a painful grimace.

An attendant entered the dining room, pushing an elegant carriage on whose embroidered pillows a young woman sat upright; blonde and extremely vivacious, she was nodding and waving to people on every side.

She was accompanied by a tall, swarthy young man on crutches.

Her carriage came to a stop at the front row of tables and the young man sat down next to her.

'Who is this lady?' asked Emanuel.

His neighbour adjusted her mirror to see where he was pointing.

'Ah, yes... that's Madame Wandeska, a Polish lady who's been at the sanatorium for almost a year. She is cured now, she's begun to walk again... The disease attacked her knee very badly. She ought to have gone home a while ago, but she keeps procrastinating...'

'Why?' Emanuel's father inquired curiously.

'Hmm. That's difficult to explain to a healthy person. Her knee healed but it froze up and became rigid. She limps when she walks. She'd prefer to remain here among the sick, where everyone has something wrong with them, than become an object of curiosity among the healthy. But she can't stay here forever… she will have to return to her family. The cure is just as merciless as the disease…'

They began to eat. The patients picked up their plates of soup with cautious movements and placed them on their chests. Emanuel too was forced to eat this way. His father sat beside him and held his plate for a while. Then, when he saw that Emanuel was beginning to get used to it, he let him eat by himself. Each time he swallowed the plate seemed about to lose its balance and tip over. It was a real acrobatic trick to perform, but the veteran patients fed themselves with such dexterity that they no longer had to pay attention to what they were doing and went on casually talking to each other.

In the front row Madame Wandeska was laughing, highly amused by the young man next to her.

'Is he the lady's husband?' Emanuel asked, pointing to the young man in the mirror.

'Tonio? Oh, no! He is a friend of hers… an Argentine… He's been well for a long time too, but prefers the air of the sanatorium to that of his law office…'

At that moment, a patient at the far end of the dining room dropped his cutlery with a loud clatter. His carriage was low enough that if he had reached out slightly with his arm, he could have picked it up. Emanuel noticed, however, that the patient stared at it without making any effort to move. A serving girl hurried up to him with another set of cutlery.

'Why didn't he pick it up himself? It would have been easy enough…' said Emanuel.

'You think it would have been easy? He would certainly have tipped over; he's wearing a corset weighing dozens of kilos.'

Emanuel was stupefied. He could see very well that the patient lay rigid on his carriage, yet nothing had made him suspect that the man was wearing a corset under his suit.

'Dr Cériez does it brilliantly, doesn't he?' added the young lady. 'It's impossible to make out the shape of the cast beneath the clothes… They're tailor made.'

She drummed her fingers on her dress, and the sound as she hit something solid underneath it was hard and dry. She too wore a corset; yet she was fully dressed from head to toe, with no external indication of the infirmity she suffered.

'I'm having a cast made myself,' said Emanuel with great despondency in his voice.

Now, as he stared at the sprawling rows of patients, his illness was no longer a simple matter of an abstract phrase, 'being ill' as opposed to 'being healthy'. He felt as if he had joined the ranks of a military hierarchy. He was part of the fellowship of illness, the fellowship of the plaster cast… His own body, stretched out on its trolley, had assumed the precise, motionless position of an invalid…

The meal was almost over when Ernest hurried in, accompanied by another patient. Ernest walked normally; the other paused for an instant in the doorway, calculating with his eyes the distance that separated him from his table, as if summoning up the strength to cross the dining room.

But here was a new and painful surprise. What was this? The walk of a cripple, the performance of a masquerade, the routine of a clown?

The patient supported himself on two walking canes. With each step, he flung a leg violently into the air. He held it for a second suspended and quaking, then swung it to the side and set it down, still quaking, on the parquet floor. It was such a convulsive means of movement, so unarticulated and inhuman, that no clown in the world could have succeeded in mimicking it. It was as if he was leaping, but no one ever leapt like this. An epileptic fit, that was it: a true epileptic fit of the legs.

Meanwhile Ernest appeared to be searching for someone; he seemed to care little about the meal; when he spotted Emanuel, he came rushing towards him.

'Are you the new patient Dr Cériez has been telling me about?' he asked, introducing himself. His movements were jerky, almost savage. A devouring curiosity burned in his eyes. 'Do you know your fellow diners?' was his next question.

The patient to the right tore his eyes from his book for an instant, cross at having been interrupted.

'Let me introduce you to Monsieur Roger Torn…' Ernest went on. 'A good friend of Mlle Cora.'

And he pointed to the patient in the blue dress to whom Emanuel had been talking. Both Roger Torn and Cora turned bright red.

'How insufferable you are!' the young girl reproached him.

'Yes, so you think…' said Ernest. 'But I believe you will soon see things differently… I know how to take care of it…' he added with a sly wink.

Ernest went off to eat. A newspaper boy came in and started handing out papers and magazines. The patients turned over the pages and began to read. The meal was over and the attendants now came to wheel the trolleys one by one into the garden. As for Emanuel, ever since he had seen the man with the convulsive legs, he had been overcome by a great and terrible sadness. Emanuel watched the servants pushing the trolleys with a heavy heart. This contrast between leading an apparently normal life (reading the newspaper, sharing meals in a restaurant, being fully dressed), this contrast between being a man like other men and yet lying imprisoned in a cast with tuberculosis eating away at your bones, that was what was so painful and sad about this illness. That was where the paradox lay: in existing, and yet not being 'fully alive'…

He left the dining room in bewilderment. Behind him the conversations and the din continued, full of animation. The serving girls gathered up the cutlery and plates, smiling at the patients as they passed.

Ernest came up to him to suggest a promenade in a horse and carriage that very afternoon.

'These beautiful autumn days are numbered here at Berck,' he said. 'The rain will soon be keeping us imprisoned indoors.'

Emanuel accepted gladly.

5

'YOU KNOW, FOR me personally, the disease doesn't seem so horrible…' Emanuel confided to Ernest as they waited in his room for someone to let them know when their carriages were ready.

'I have always had a core of idleness in me, which now turns out to be completely satisfied,' he went on. 'I stretch my bones out on my trolley, I'm wonderfully rested, I feel great… And I have no desire to walk… I think if I got up, the pain in my back would be merciless. Only one thing disturbs me…'

His father, who had been sitting on the bed and apparently reading the newspaper, abruptly raised his head.

'I am disturbed by the thought that little by little I will be forced to become a true invalid… That what now seems like idleness and rest will soon become a terrible imprisonment… I'm afraid of things deteriorating… I'm scared I'll end up walking with two canes and leaping like a frog.'

'Yes, but look at me! I was cured,' Ernest reassured him, pounding a fist on his chest.

'You wear a corset too?' Emanuel asked.

His chest had sounded hard.

'Yes… but it's just a simple corset, not one made of plaster,' Ernest replied half-heartedly.

'May I see?'

Ernest took off his jacket and shirt. He resembled an ancient warrior encased in his cuirass, or a mechanical bust, full of screws and belts, on show in an orthopaedic display case. The corset kept his body rigid from hip to shoulder. It was made of pink celluloid, perforated with thousands of tiny holes and tied with laces at the back. It was screwed together around the neck, the hips and up the sides, by means of a highly complicated apparatus made of nickel alloy.

'So how long will you have to wear it?' asked Emanuel.

'We shall never be parted from each other,' Ernest answered. 'I only take it off at night to go to bed… I'll always have to wear it… Maybe my whole life…'

Emanuel became pensive. 'Well, if I have to go back to the real world hermetically sealed in that contraption, I'd rather…'

He left the sentence unfinished, and the room went quiet. His father sank back into his newspaper while Ernest put his shirt and jacket back on.

After a few minutes, his father stopped reading and began

packing his suitcase. He was leaving that very afternoon. From the uneasy silence of everyone in the room, it was clear that Emanuel's unfinished words were still having an effect.

'Don't do anything stupid,' his father said while packing his things and avoiding Emanuel's gaze. 'I'll send you money so you can take care of yourself… so you can get well… I will work for you… just for you… don't ever forget that.'

Emanuel was prone to easily changing emotions. Listening to his father speak with such feeling, he was momentarily in tears, but a second later he forgot everything and rang impatiently to ask about their carriage.

Eventually a boy came to announce that the carriage was ready to go. The suitcase was ready too – nothing remained but for them all to go downstairs.

Awaiting them in the courtyard was a kind of enormous horse-drawn boat on wheels with a canvas covering. Was this a carriage for the patients? Yes, that's exactly what it was. Emanuel didn't need to move at all. The mattress and frame on which he was lying went in at the back, where his stretcher-bed slid in on rollers as into a hearse. The attendant closed the back panel and handed Ernest the reins. Emanuel lay with his back slightly raised so that he could see ahead without obstruction. His father and Ernest sat next to him on two little seats. There was plenty of room for the suitcase; in fact, there was enough room for the cargo of a sailing ship…

The sunny, cold days of autumn were coming to an end. The grass in the gardens was drying up and the feeble afternoon light rustled quietly through the red, crumpled leaves on the trees.

The streets seemed abandoned… Emanuel's gaze drifted along the unfamiliar houses, the villas with their awnings drawn down, in that little town lost somewhere in the world under the hazy autumn sky.

At the far end of one street he suddenly caught sight of the immense brilliance of the sea… In it floated the fantastic shadows of fishing boats, far off amid gold and light.

Emanuel took hold of the reins and drove by himself straight on towards the beach.

There were wooden ramps that sloped very gently down from the esplanade directly onto the sand. There were some other carriages there, huddled in a circle. Patients were carrying on conversations, shouting from one carriage to another. One was playing the mandolin; a woman patient was knitting.

The ocean sparkled, nothing but crystal and azure. Emanuel breathed in that inexpressible fullness of immense luminosity – the vast expanse of the air, the infinity of water.

His father and Ernest had gone for a short walk. In about an hour the train would leave. Emanuel was content to be left alone. He filled his chest with deep breaths, following with his eyes the leisurely course of the black sailboats. For a moment he experienced a huge sense of abandon. But in a short time the other two returned and his quiet ecstasy evaporated.

'We only have another half-hour together,' his father said, filled with emotion.

Emanuel now drove the carriage toward the train station, along a large street fronted with huge shop windows, and vaguely enlivened by a few passers-by. He was seeing it for the first time and yet it seemed as if it was somehow already known to him. He felt that he now belonged to this street, to the ocean whose light he had breathed in, to this foreign autumn, far more than to his father. A perception of the world had been overturned within him, and a certain sense of familiarity had shifted from one pan of the scales to the other. The street held an old nostalgia, a memory. Perhaps he had seen it once in a dream…

The parting was quick and simple.

They had dawdled on the way and now they had no more than a minute before the train left.

His father embraced him hastily and staggered out of sight. He carried away with him, like an unbearable weight in his soul, the melancholy of this over-hasty separation.

Emanuel, left alone, experienced a brief moment of hesitation. He was now facing an unfamiliar and daunting life. What was he supposed to do? What was going to happen to him? There are ordinary moments of existence, mundane intervals of solitude, that can occur anywhere, when the world's atmosphere suddenly transforms, abruptly acquiring a new meaning, heavier and more exhausting.

'You are sad, it seems,' Ernest said when he returned from the platform. 'Why didn't your father stay another day or two?'

Emanuel, his thoughts in a jumble, had no reply. Ernest took over the reins and drove them through unfamiliar streets. Rows of houses passed by his gaze, roofs… windows… window after window… intimate, old-fashioned provincial gardens with their bright bouquets of geraniums…

Ernest interrupted his reverie.

'Did you notice that Roger Torn is furious at you?'

'Who's Roger Torn?'

'Your table-mate on the right... you know... in the dining room, the red-haired patient with his head buried in a book.'

'Aha! Yes! I know who you mean... And you say he's furious at me? What have I done to him?' asked Emanuel in bewilderment.

'Strictly speaking, you did nothing... it's not your fault at all... But that's how things turned out. Before you came here, Roger Torn and Mlle Cora always sat at the same table... It's an old understanding between them. The sanatorium director never misses a chance to cause trouble: he placed you between them to keep them apart.'

'And what can I do about it now?' asked Emanuel. 'I suppose I can ask for another place in the dining room...'

Ernest thought for a second. 'Yes, that would be the best thing. Tell the director you want to sit next to me...'

That very afternoon, as soon as they were back, Emanuel asked to be taken to the director's office, a gloomy little room with a shiny, paperless desk. The single object sitting on it was a telephone. The director sat behind it with his head leaning on his hand, like a well-fed dog behind his half-eaten bone. He listened to Emanuel's request with acerbic, professional benevolence. 'Yes, it's possible... I will give instructions for the places to be changed,' he said, beginning to smile; but his smile slipped into the grimace of someone who has bitten off much more food than he can swallow.

That evening, Roger Torn and Cora were reunited at their table; Cora gaved Emanuel a little wave of thanks.

'You see, I'm not quite so insufferable, am I?' said Ernest to her in passing.

And when he came to Emanuel's table: 'To celebrate the reconciliation, tomorrow evening at nine, a society soirée… a ball, in my room…'

6

EMANUEL WAS TIRED. He had put himself to bed, and had been lying there for a long while when someone knocked at the door. He had spent the day inside with a few other patients. It had rained the whole time, a cold and gloomy rain with sharp gusts of wind that drove the water against the windows. A dreadful silence and sense of isolation reigned throughout the sanatorium.

'Who's there?'

'Were you asleep? Can we come in? We're here to fetch you...'

It was Ernest, accompanied by Tonio, the tall Argentine, Madame Wandeska's friend.

Emanuel had forgotten about the party; to be honest he had taken Ernest's invitation as a joke. 'You can see I'm in my pyjamas. I'm sorry but I have to say no...'

'Hey, don't be a spoilsport... As if you're the only one in pyjamas...' said Tonio.

Ernest wasn't fully dressed either, all he had on was a shirt and a pair of trousers. His corset glistened strangely around his neck in the weak light that came from the corridor. Tonio wore a thoroughly exotic, flowery dressing gown. This evening he supported himself with only a walking stick.

'Look at us! Do we look like we're dressed for a ball? Come on, don't be a bore,' insisted Ernest.

Emanuel had no choice. Ernest and Tonio wheeled his trolley out of the door. Ernest's room was on the same corridor, but on the other side of the building, facing the street.

It might have been ten o'clock. Everybody in the sanatorium was asleep. They made their way along the corridor in silence. A single anaemic light bulb lit the entire floor.

'Slowly! Watch out... We're banging into all the doors,' whispered Ernest in annoyance. 'The management might have bothered to put another light bulb in the corridor...'

'One light bulb?' Tonio muttered sarcastically, 'Why only one light bulb? They ought to have the whole place lit up...'

A low, muffled murmur of voices could be heard coming from Ernest's room.

Emanuel's entrance was greeted with applause.

'This is our new friend and the management's latest acquisition!'

Unbelievable chaos and confusion reigned in the room. A few stretcher-beds with their respective patients had been pushed over to the window, while other guests were standing up. Emanuel recognised Roger Torn and Cora, their trolleys intimately conjoined. In the corner by the window lay a portly, dark-skinned man with an aquiline nose, calmly smoking a pipe. Emanuel suspected that this was Zed. Ernest had talked about him a great deal the day before. He was a former racing car driver. Everybody called him Zed because in his racing days he used to wear that letter on his jersey. He had won a formidable number of trophies until one day he had an accident that shattered both his feet below the ankle. Now he lay on a stretcher-bed, with a blanket that covered a large object at his feet. Ernest had explained that Zed's feet were confined in a plaster block and that bits of the toes and skin were held together by silver pins. 'A real meat hash!' Ernest had concluded.

There was another man in the room who was talking to Zed and two young girls. In addition a patient from another clinic was lying on a stretcher-bed near them. He was called Valentin and had a terribly insignificant face.

Ernest made introductions. One of the girls, Katty, was Irish.

'Katty, in brief…' began Ernest. 'Credentials not completely established… twenty-one years old… came to Berck to study the patients, the way other girls her age go to Italy to study works of art…'

Katty laughed loudly. She was clearly a little drunk. Her reddish hair was thoroughly dishevelled, and her face blowsy and freckled, like a garishly made-up mannequin.

Ernest began to pour white wine into a bowl for a fruit punch. He was assisted by the other girl, a quiet and serious blonde with delicate, simple gestures.

Emanuel stared, his eyes riveted on her as she quickly and deftly peeled the bananas and apples.

Ernest had not introduced her, but Emanuel was looking at her with such insistence that the girl noticed, blushed and mumbled, somewhat confusedly:

'I'm Solange...' She dried herself with a towel and held out her hand to him.

When the punch was ready, Katty was about to pour it out into glasses.

'One moment!' said Ernest. There was a drop of rum left in a bottle, which he poured into the bowl.

The punch was very strong. They all had wineglasses; only Tonio and Zed asked for large tumblers. The potency of the drink and the thick smoke that wafted through the room made Emanuel fairly lightheaded. He saw the whole crowd of people through a foggy, alcoholic haze. And that silvery, melodious name – Solange – persisted in his mind like an additional, gentle intoxication.

'This is a tonic for women who've fainted,' Tonio protested. 'Come on, Ernest! Don't you have anything else?'

'Cognac, if you want it. But pure cognac, and that's not to be messed with. It goes down your throat like hot lava...'

'Let's see about that!' said Tonio.

Ernest brought two bottles and began to uncork one of them.

'What do you say, Zed?' shouted Tonio across the room, 'How about a race, over the distance of a bottle of cognac? Come on, quickly, answer...'

'Against the clock or starting together?'

Zed took things like a true professional.

'Starting together!'

Ernest uncorked a second bottle and gave one to each contestant. Everyone's eyes were now fixed on them. 'Three... two... one!' counted Ernest.

Zed raised his bottle to his lips at the same moment as Tonio. There were a few sonorous glugs, then Tonio threw his empty bottle on the bed. He had drunk it in three gulps, as if he were dying of thirst.

'It's pretty clear you're in love...' said someone.

Who had spoken? With a fixed stare and uncertain movements, Tonio picked up a glass of wine from the table and brought it to his lips. For a moment the room was silent. But Valentin, the patient next to him, was in a talkative mood. He had not spoken before but now he opened his mouth and started blathering moronically.

'Come on – as if we don't all know you're in love with Madame Wandeska?' the idiot insisted excitably.

This time Tonio was dumbfounded.

For a few moments he stared about him, at each and every person, imploring for help, as if to say, look at this snotty-nosed kid who's making fun of me!

Suddenly he raised his glass and began speaking in a solemn voice that was almost a shout: 'Honoured guests... all... all you... who are here, I declare this evening... on my conscience and on my honour that between me and Madame Wandeska there isn't any sort of... relationship. We are friends... that's all... do you hear me?'

He had completely lost his head. Valentin was obviously also drunk, because he wouldn't shut up.

'Hee, hee, hee!' he cackled. 'As if we didn't know you go to her room every night.'

'Yes, to talk, you animal! To talk!' shouted Tonio. 'Don't you know that Madame Wandeska wears a cast… down to her calf…? Her entire leg is in a cast… what kind of love can you make in that condition?'

He spoke with great hesitation in his voice; it was clear that his conscience tormented him for making these declarations in public, but he couldn't control his drunkenness.

'So what if she's in a cast,' continued Valentin. 'As if you couldn't make love in a cast! You fondle her… you kiss her… in all sorts of places…'

Tonio walked up to him, gnashing his teeth. He stared into Valentin's eyes for a moment before abruptly emptying the contents of the glass he was holding into his face.

Valentin, stunned, his face sopping wet, began to wipe himself with his hands. Then, when he had recovered a little, he snatched a jug violently from the dressing table and took aim at Tonio's head.

'Hey, hey, let's avoid any criminal activity if we can!' shouted Ernest as he pushed his way between them.

'You, Tonio, lie down here…' he ordered as he wrestled him down onto the bed. 'Stay there like a good boy and meditate quietly on your cognac.'

At the same time he wheeled Valentin's trolley to the middle of the room, away from the Argentine.

'What an animal! What an animal!' grumbled Tonio, stretching out on the bed clothes. 'If Ernest hadn't got between us, I would have given him four good slaps and left him dead on the spot!'

'No one dies from being slapped four times,' announced Zed calmly from his corner, like an impartial referee in the match.

In order to create a diversion, Ernest began quietly humming a tune. All the others joined in the chorus:

'Votre mari… bididi… bididi…

Il est dans la soupente…'

'Not so loud! Not so loud!' cried Ernest.

'En train de baiser bididi… bididi…'

Ernest heaved a comical sigh and everyone started laughing.

'En train de baiser la servante…'

It was a miserable dirge, full of drunken obscenities… Instead of reviving and animating them, the song plunged them further into torpor. Outside, the rain drummed on the windows, the wind whistled its fierce, long lament.

Everyone in the room was shut in a state of stupor, as if silently consumed by some profound inner preoccupation. Katty threw herself down on the bed next to Tonio and ran her fingers through his hair, gently comforting him.

'Hey, don't worry, it'll pass… Tonio… Tononio… Tonononio…'

'What's that?' Tonio asked thickly.

'That's how we talked "Chinese" at school,' said Katty in a childish voice.

Valentin began to recite verses but was suddenly interrupted by a dispute that broke out between Zed and the man next to him. The man was an engineer from Paris who came to Berck from time to time on vacation in order to take a rest cure and shoot wild duck in the Authie Estuary, which is famous for it.

'And I'm telling you, I could hit it with a single shot,' the engineer insisted.

He pointed with his finger at something through the window.

'All right, turn off the lights,' ordered Zed. 'It's easier to see in the dark…'

Now the room was dark, flickering reflections came through the window from a streetlight swaying in the wind.

'I'll have it first go…'

'We'll see… we'll see,' said Zed calmly.

They had made a wager between themselves as to whether the engineer would hit the bulb of the streetlight with his gun.

'I think you've gone completely mad, both of you!' said Solange, frightened.

The engineer left the room and came back a few minutes later with something heavy in his hands. Ernest was half-asleep in the dark and not fully aware of what was going on, until the engineer opened the window and a cold blast of wind and rain gusted into the room, scattering everything about.

Ernest, wide awake now, staggered to the window.

'Do you really want to do that? Have you all gone crazy tonight?'

But he was too late. The engineer had brought the gun to his eye, taken aim and fired. The shot resounded dramatically, everyone was horrified. Surely the entire sanatorium must have been woken.

What would happen now? Everyone was shaking with alarm and agitation. Tonio had started out of his sleep in bewilderment and was emptying the entire contents of his stomach with horrible retching noises.

In the street the bulb continued to burn, buffeted by the wind. Ernest was struggling in vain to shut the window, while Solange tried to wrest the gun from Zed, who had taken it from the engineer.

He was absolutely determined to use it and nothing was going to prevent him.

'If you don't let go of the gun, I'll shoot into the ceiling! My finger's on the trigger,' Zed declared fiercely. He was already sitting up in his stretcher-bed, with his chest in the air, aiming at the light bulb outside.

Ernest got out of the way as the second shot resounded even louder, more terrible, more terrifying than the first. The whole event, both shots, had lasted less than a minute. In the street the bulb had gone out: a bull's eye.

Everyone in the room was too shocked to make any further protest. Zed leant the gun against a chair. Ernest closed the window slowly, with the numbed movements of someone who has endured an immense catastrophe in the face of which he was powerless to do anything. His teeth chattered from cold and from anger; he was trying to find words sharp enough, violent enough to free himself from the panic inside him, but the shots still held him crushed beneath a stupefying weight of terror.

Emanuel had witnessed the entire scene with the vivid impression that none of it was taking place in reality. For the last few minutes, ever since the fight between Tonio and Valentin, everything around him had acquired an unintelligible, artificial character. Were these people real? It seemed as if he was attending a ridiculously unrealistic and pointless performance. Would the cast manage to remain in character and keep a straight face to the end?

Rather than bringing him back to his senses, the gunshots plunged him deeper into incomprehension and hallucination. The blasts were the *coup de grâce* that shattered reality and plunged it into the darkness of night. What would unfold from now on could only be weak and feeble, like a world made of rags and cotton wool. Emanuel was powerless to imagine what would follow. Anything could happen now…

Zed was mumbling on breathlessly: 'You saw how I hit it? An invalid I may be, but still a man… Ha! Ha! Look at me, all smashed up as I am, I still outdid a real hunter… Ha! Ha!…'

He asked for another drink. His inebriation had become that sorry earnestness with which drunks obstinately persist in doing absurd things.

Ernest didn't know what to do with himself and paced back and forth round the room. 'What'll we do now? What's going to happen? The director will throw us all out tomorrow… What insanity!'

Ever since the gunshots, doors could be heard opening and closing throughout the sanatorium, along with whispering and footsteps up and down the corridor. Ernest went and put his ear to the door. Somewhere at the far end of a corridor a door slammed noisily.

'It's the director! He's coming to investigate! What am I going to tell him?'

Everyone was waiting, breathless with intense anticipation.

'Please, quiet now! Complete and utter quiet...' The sound of shuffling feet could be heard coming toward the room.

Ernest slowly turned the key in the lock. 'Quiet,' he whispered. 'I thought it was the director, but...'

Someone knocked on the door. Absolute silence reigned in the room.

'Open the door! Come on, open up, Monsieur Ernest! What's going on in there? What have you been up to?'

It was the high-pitched, reedy voice of an old woman. She began rattling the door and squawking like a bird.

'Open up! Open the door!'

'What's the matter? Who's there?' Ernest asked from inside the room.

'Open up, Monsieur Ernest, or I'll call the attendants to break the door down... It's me, the night supervisor... Come on, open up!'

'And what exactly do you want from me?' Ernest asked, quite calmly.

'You're asking me what I want? You go drinking, you get drunk, you shoot guns... What is this place, a sanatorium or a drinking den?'

'A whorehouse,' Ernest exclaimed, unperturbed.

And then he in turn started shouting.

'What do you want? Who sent you? Who's shooting guns? Have you gone crazy? Look here, I only woke up when I heard the shots myself... Somebody shot a gun in the street... what am I supposed to do, play the policeman? Go and see who shot the gun... and leave me in peace.'

Someone in the next room pounded on the wall, objecting to the row.

'The shots came from here!' the high-pitched voice outside the door obstinately insisted. 'I'm going to get the director…'

Ernest turned the key in the lock and with a sudden movement opened the door wide. He was now face to face with the supervisor: he, tall and broad-shouldered, she a little frail old woman in a white uniform, a skeletal apparition in the pale light of the corridor, an emaciated phantom in the dead of night.

'Listen. What do you want? Tell me loud and clear, what do you want? Why did you make a beeline for my room? I'm always the scapegoat in this sanatorium… When someone pours wine in the piano in the hall – you go to Ernest: Ernest poured it… When there is too much noise somewhere – straight to Ernest… When someone shoots a gun, Ernest… always Ernest. Please tell the director that tomorrow I am leaving this place. I've had enough… do you hear me?'

The supervisor stood rooted to the spot and speechless in bewilderment beneath this sudden avalanche of arguments. Ernest protested with such vehemence and sincerity that one could only be filled with pity for such a persecuted young man.

The supervisor, totally stymied, had no idea now how to extricate herself from the situation.

'Well… all right, all right… I'll go and see the sergeant down the street,' she mumbled in confusion and shuffled off along the corridor, to the accompaniment of the clinking of the keys on her chain.

Ernest turned triumphantly to face the room.

'You see? If you want to frighten that old crone, tell her you're leaving the sanatorium. She's been working here for forty years and the routine sticks to her... like mould sticks to the walls...'

It was going to be more difficult to get all the patients back to their rooms now, and besides Ernest was exhausted, his back hurt, and there was no question of Tonio helping him. He had fallen asleep again in his acrid, stinking heap of undigested food. For the time being they all decided to stay in the room and sleep as best they could, and at dawn they could slip a few francs to an attendant to take everyone back clandestinely.

Outside the rain had stopped. Ernest opened the window a little to let out the heavy reek of wine and cigarettes. Zed slept with his mouth open and forming a perfect O, as if even in sleep he was still amazed at the accuracy of his shot.

Emanuel couldn't see Roger and Cora but suspected he could tell where their stretcher-beds were lying side-by-side from their passionate whispers and the various squeaks of the trolley springs.

In the light of a match that Ernest had struck in order to find the water jug, Roger and Cora appeared for an instant, lying on their sides, embracing each other.

'They rub their casts against each other. That's all they can do,' whispered Ernest in Emanuel's ear.

And Solange? Where was Solange?

Emanuel found her by the window, looking out into the night. Outside, the darkness was growing more threadbare and patchy, and Emanuel strained to determine her exact silhouette against the background. The room had become entirely still.

'Move over a bit more, you animal!' Ernest gave Tonio a shove and lay down in turn next to Katty.

Valentin was fast asleep, breathing loudly and thinly through his nose. His snoring settled over the quiet of the room like a web of sound weaving itself over the prostrate bodies… Emanuel wasn't aware of when he fell asleep, his eyes still fixed on the window, on the uncertain spot that was Solange.

He woke up at dawn in a state of confusion, not so much tired as distressed. An acrid morning-after melancholy pervaded the room. The atmosphere of the 'soirée' had atrophied into the stuffy grey air and the desolate clarity of a sunless morning.

Solange had long since left. Katty and Tonio too. Ernest and an attendant were currently struggling with Mlle Cora's carriage.

As soon as she was out of the room, Roger Torn lifted the blanket that covered him and examined his mattress.

'Oh hell!' he blurted out miserably. 'My entire mattress is wet, and my pyjamas and all…'

He had open fistulae and more than likely had not been well bandaged.

'What? What is it?' asked Valentin, sounding hungover. 'Did it get through?'

'Yes… and there's even more of it… what a mess! I'll have to lie in this sauce till eight when the clinic opens…'

From where he was Emanuel could see the bedsheets covered in a greenish, purulent liquid.

Ernest and the attendant returned and joined in the contemplation of the disaster.

'If you will go frolicking around all night long!' said Ernest. 'Serve you right!'

'Hey, spare me, please, the lecture on morality at five in the morning,' replied Roger Torn bitterly.

It was now Emanuel's turn to go; he waved goodbye to the others. Ernest pushed his trolley out, and yawned as wide as his mouth would open.

Emanuel found himself alone once more in his room, and the daylight appeared to him even more forsaken... more desolate... A cruel emptiness had been hollowed out in his breast, like a deep need to breathe, or to weep.

7

EMANUEL WOULD HAVE slept till lunchtime if he had not received an unexpected visit.

He opened his eyes wide as Dr Cériez walked in, attended by two nurses.

'He's bound to be here to scold me for last night's party,' he thought. He wasn't looking forward to being taken to task while lying down, with nowhere to look while the doctor stared at him from above, and no way of escaping from his humiliating position, stretched out on his trolley like an animal ready for dissection.

'Still asleep so late in the morning?' asked the doctor in his deep, jovial voice.

His friendly demeanour tortured Emanuel. He felt he was burning under the sheets.

'Are you ready for some unpleasant news on a gloomy day like today?' the doctor went on in his affable manner.

'He probably wants to tell me he's throwing me out of the clinic,' imagined Emanuel, and he quickly lifted his head, attempting a carefree smile and roguish air.

'Well, let me tell you why I'm here. I want to ask you if you'd like me to put you into your cast today. Sooner or later you'll have to wear it. The vertebrae need to be secured if you want the damaged bit to heal. What do you say? Shall we do it now, or wait one more day?'

Emanuel let out a sigh of relief; he was so thankful there was no talk of the party that he gave no thought to the cast and immediately replied effusively: 'Of course, today... certainly... do it! I think I've already got used to lying down, so I'll cope with the rest easily enough...'

'You're the first patient who's been happy to receive his cast,' the doctor smiled. 'Generally when I say that, the other patients look as if they're about to faint.'

An attendant wheeled him to the clinic.

In the antiseptic white room, amidst the orthopaedic equipment, Emanuel's heart abruptly tightened, and in a sudden reckoning of sincerity, he regretted his previous enthusiasm.

'In any case, better a plaster cast than a lecture on morality,' he encouraged himself darkly. His thoughts were in something of a tangle and the only clear and intelligible thing around him was the strong reek of phenol.

Eva, the nurse, removed his pyjamas.

'That was one hell of a party,' she murmured in a low voice

so that the doctor did not hear her.

She liked to become intimate with the patients and affect friendship. But on the other hand, she gossiped about them all to the doctor. Ernest had observed her many times shuttling spurious information back and forth. Emanuel pretended not to understand what she was talking about.

In any case, the doctor was ready and wanted to start. He had put on a long gown, buttoned all the way to the neck, and rubber boots to protect him from being spattered with the plaster.

The temperature in the clinic was rather cold.

'You'll be warm enough very soon,' whispered Eva bitchily, irritated at Emanuel's rejection of her affability.

She dressed him in a thin white cotton shirt, like a sports shirt. Emanuel saw his reflection in the convex surface of a nickel-plated box and found it suited him rather well.

'You'll be wearing that all the time from now on, till the cast comes off,' said the doctor.

The rapture faded instantly.

They stretched him out face down on two tables attached to each other. Then they detached the tables, leaving Emanuel with his torso suspended over the gap, making a bridge between them.

On chairs nearby, bowls containing white powder, steaming water and strips of cloth stood ready and waiting.

The procedure itself was not at all complicated: the doctor took a strip of cloth, rolled it in plaster and dowsed it in water. Then he applied it lengthwise across Emanuel's back like a compress. Slap! The first one... Slap! Another one... The strips of cloth glued themselves to his ribs, his chest... his hips... they clung to the skin like living things, sticky little animals, snuggling up to him. The doctor worked with the deft speed of a bricklayer out of whose hands the bricks seem to be flying. He quickly oozed the plaster out with his palms, pressed it lightly and shaped it to Emanuel's body. The strips flopped down one after the other and enveloped Emanuel in a white tunic from his neck to his hips.

He did indeed begin to feel warm. The process was neither disagreeable nor painful. Inside the corset a lukewarm dampness was gluing itself to him, not unpleasantly, and from time to time a trickle of water ran down from his shoulders onto his back, making him quiver with its delicate, tactile calligraphy.

Now his back was ready. The plaster had to be reinforced on his chest, and it had already begun to harden.

'Let's see, can you roll onto your back by yourself?' asked the doctor, pushing the tables back together.

'Yes… right away…' Emanuel answered impetuously and, supporting himself on a corner of the table, tried to turn his body.

What was going on? He was stunned. How many tons did he weigh now? Impossible to move. He lay inert, his whole strength cancelled out, a prisoner in a corset. That was it, then!

The shell held him hermetically sealed, immobile, overpowered, crushed as if by a boulder. 'Farewell, Emanuel!' he told himself. 'You've turned into a dead man,' and a painful knot rose in his throat.

'What's to be done now?' he asked.

The nurse and the doctor turned him on his back. They

manoeuvred him like a lifeless mannequin. They lifted him, turned him over, and put him down carefully on the table so as not to bruise him. Emanuel, dispossessed of all his normal movements, had a horrid sensation of annihilation only experienced before in dreams.

The doctor clipped off a square in the stomach area in order to leave him free to breathe.

He rounded off the corset with scissors around the pubis and hips. When Emanuel lifted his head a little to take a look at the whole length of his body, he discovered he had become an entirely hybrid statue, a strange combination of flesh and plaster.

They wheeled him back to his room. The nurse brought hot water bottles to aid the drying process. Outside an insistent drizzle began drumming once more on the windows. The radiator came on and the hot water bottles were placed around the plaster. The previously agreeable warmth of the compresses had now deteriorated, at the smallest attempt at movement on Emanuel's part, into a humid squelching inside the corset. He lay with his head back, staring at the cracks in the ceiling. As time passed, the plaster hardened and the dampness became increasingly cold. The warmth of the water bottles was unable to penetrate beneath the plaster. Some food was brought to him but he left it untouched. What good was it stuffing food into this plaster box?

Ernest came to see him straight after lunch.

'You've got your uniform! You're a member of the order!' he exclaimed. 'And they got you right after our party. I hope you'd come to your senses.'

He stretched out on the bed next to the trolley and lit a cigarette.

'Zed and that engineer of his – they're insane! That affair could have turned into a serious scandal...'

Emanuel tried to remember the previous night in Ernest's room, but now, in the light of the rainy afternoon, in the quiet underscored by the low wheezing of the radiator, all the precise details of the evening had vanished into a calm despair. It was as if nothing had ever taken place, as if nothing had ever existed except the cold and soggy binding of the corset.

Ernest followed the sinuous trickling of the water as it streaked the windows. He too was demoralised by the autumn day.

'I like the rain...' he said at length. 'This is fitting weather for us patients. Rain, gloomy sky, cold... You realise the entire world is reduced to the same four-walled room... to the same sadness.'

Emanuel understood with his whole heart.

'When the weather is fine, when it's warm and sunny,' continued Ernest, 'then everything appears horribly useless and senseless. What can a man do amid bright, sunny surroundings? And even if he could do something... it's too obvious... too visible, too intelligible. Perhaps the most disturbing mysteries are the ones where the evidence is plainest for us to see. I like these dark and rainy days best, when you curl up in your room and feel like a dog that's been beaten...'

They sat in silence for a while listening to the rain. Emanuel closed his eyes.

'Do you want me to leave you to sleep?'

'I couldn't... I'm lying in a horrid puddle. It's as if the dampness is getting under my skin… into my bones… into my heart… It's as if it's slowly creeping into my brain…'

Ernest agreed. 'Indeed, it's very unpleasant. I know, I know what it's like. It'll take another two or three days till it dries up… then you won't even feel it.'

The thought of two or three days filled Emanuel with horror.

'Do you think I'll ever get used to it?' he asked, pounding furiously on his shell. 'Every time I make a move, the plaster is going to keep me pinned in place and remind me that I'm hermetically sealed inside it.'

'You'll get used to it… you'll get used to it; you'll move to your heart's content… you'll see – you'll move with your plaster and all, as if it were only a shirt…'

Ernest stood up to leave.

'I want to ask you something,' said Emanuel. 'Who is that tall girl – the blonde one in your room last night? Her name is Solange.'

'Ah, Solange! She's a former patient too. She lay on a stretcher-bed just like you. You see, she got well – admirably so. But she is not a "Mademoiselle"… she's "Madame"… She was married once, and when she fell ill, her husband left her. A nice, elegant thing to do, wouldn't you say?'

'So then, what is she doing here in Berck?'

'This is the strange thing. Berck is more than just a town for invalids. It's a very subtle poison. It gets into your blood. Anyone who has lived here can't settle anywhere else in the world. One day you'll discover that too. All the shopkeepers, all the doctors, the pharmacists, even the attendants… all of them are former patients who can't live anywhere else.'

'And Solange?' Emanuel asked again in order to return to the subject that was burning within him.

'She lives alone here. She supports herself. She's a typist in a law office.'

Ernest opened the door. Emanuel held him back.

'Would I be able to speak to her? To see her?'

'Aha! We're talking about something serious! Have you fallen in love with her? That's also something I know a bit about... It's like the cast, only the opposite: a dry, burning misery. I think tomorrow I will speak to her and ask her to come. Maybe she'll come. Goodbye!'

And he left Emanuel, waterlogged, alone and full of impatience.

8

During the night the dampness became a cloak of fever and nightmares. Each time Emanuel lapsed into sleep for a moment, he plunged into a swamp. It was a winter day, sunny, with snow melting on the roof. He waded through water in his galoshes, but in the street the sun was shining.

Sun! Sun! Like fireballs flashing in all directions! A firework display – but in the light of day, in the snow! Blinding light! This is what Emanuel has always wanted. To walk with a girl in the sun, on a day like this. Solange. Perhaps. The violets still wet from the fertile earth. What fragrance! Do you see those two birds, flying from roof to roof? They are our souls... The dam has burst; in shadow I will wait for the sun, and for you, Solange... In shadows all things become blue. And then the suction cups... this is how it must be… bliss must always be absorbed in shadows and suction cups… glacial, gelatinous suction cups…

Emanuel woke up and turned on the light.

In places the plaster was heavy with water. Next to the ribs a neutral space emerged where his breathing could break free from time to time before quickly gluing itself again to the coldness. The electric light intensified his surroundings and increased his anguish at each and every object. Darkness was easier to bear.

In the gloom Emanuel charted a map of dampness and distress. There were jagged peaks that penetrated his bones… then, further on, vast, tranquil steppes of cold dampness… and finally, gulfs of relative serenity. Solange's image came into his mind, but it became impossible to form a memory of her clear blue gaze that was in any way separate from the disgusting mildewy clamminess around him.

He began to shiver from the cold. Then he was cold no longer, but continued to shiver from nerves.

Finally he fell asleep, overwhelmed by fatigue. He felt sleep overwhelming him, he knew that he was sleeping, that he was only sunk in an exhausted half-sleep, but had no strength left to think about these things. He floated in turgid and wearying waters…

Emanuel spent the entire morning in the hall with other patients, children, old ladies crocheting, reclining imposingly on their trolleys like Indian statues. The walls sweated a pallid, greenish paint, as if the room were suffering from a horrible, secret disease.

Shrouded up to the neck in white blankets, Emanuel could barely move his head from one side to the other.

He could see the 'Marquise', a former schoolteacher who always wore a dress of violet velvet, bracelets and rings on her fingers, and lace and pendants decorating her enormous defunct breasts.

In a corner a little boy of about ten ground the handle of a music box that produced a repetitive, maddening refrain out of the same three minor notes. He was the son of a Viennese merchant. His father sat next to him, stroking his hair.

The conversation was general. Emanuel was caught in the middle like easy prey. Everyone became interested in his cast. Emanuel responded with good-natured boredom. He was secretly racked by anticipation. Ernest had gone downstairs to telephone Solange and ask her if she could come to the sanatorium.

'In any case, she works mornings; maybe in the afternoon…' said Ernest. 'And what should I tell her? What reason should I give her?'

Emanuel thought for a moment.

'Just say that I want to see her…'

Ernest hadn't returned yet. In his impatience, Emanuel began to mix up the answers to the questions he was being asked from all directions.

'Do you have a headache?' asked the 'Marquise'.

'Yes, a horrible one… my head and my neck… the right hip too…' answered Emanuel with the utmost gravity.

After that, everyone left him alone.

Finally he heard Ernest returning.

'She's coming!' he signalled discreetly, winking slyly from the door.

Emanuel felt as if a massive weight had suddenly evaporated from his cast.

But Solange was late and did not appear until it was almost time for dinner, as the attendants were beginning to wheel the patients towards the lift. Emanuel asked to be taken to his room. Ernest and Solange followed behind him down the corridor. He experienced one of the odd sensations of his illness; that of a patient being pushed along on a stretcher-bed, followed by healthy people. There was something reminiscent of a family procession behind a corpse on a bier… or of passengers scrambling after their baggage carrier.

Emanuel would have liked to have been left alone with Solange, even if only for a moment. Ernest understood and wanted to leave but Solange made him stay.

She enquired about the cast.

'It's very unpleasant… isn't it? I was in a cast too, for eight months, and now I've forgotten all about it…'

There were no chairs in the room. Solange sat on the bed, alongside Emanuel. She was so close to him that he smelled her perfume, an indistinguishable mixture of mandarin and lavender, a fresh perfume that matched perfectly the simple jumper she wore, a blue jersey with a turned-up white collar, like a schoolgirl's. The entire grace of this young woman came from a certain severity of dress, of gesture, of scent…

They spoke about insignificant things while Emanuel endeavoured to find a way of convincing her to come and see him again, alone.

He suddenly began to moan, at first very discreetly, then increasing his moaning in intensity to the exact threshold at which the others could hear him, but at the same time think that he didn't want to be heard.

'What's the matter?' asked Solange.

Emanuel stopped moaning and frowned. He had to play this well, to make it clear that he was suffering in secret and stoically preferred to keep quiet about it.

'Oh… nothing, absolutely nothing,' said Emanuel with an effort of will that frightened his companions.

'But I can see that something is hurting you – you must tell us what it is… I won't leave till I know what's hurting you,' said Solange, with unexpected compassion.

Emanuel was exultant, but he protested again with the same melancholy tone:

'I assure you… it's nothing… it will pass…'

Solange seemed sincerely upset. 'Oh, come on, what is it…?'

'My liver,' murmured Emanuel. (He had never had any problems with his liver in his whole life.)

'Where does it hurt…? Show me…' said Ernest.

Emanuel didn't quite know where the pains resulting from an attack of the liver should be. He pointed with open palm to his entire chest and half of his belly. That would do, in his opinion.

'Oh, ho!' Ernest wondered. 'These pains are radiating out from the midriff …'

'And the pains came just as you got fitted with the cast…'

'It's horrible,' whispered Emanuel, and he felt so sincerely sorry for himself that his eyes nearly filled with tears.

'What should we do?' asked Solange.

Just then a tray of food was brought in. Emanuel was faint with hunger.

'I think it would be best not to eat anything,' advised Ernest.

'Yes… yes,' Solange agreed. 'A cup of tea, just a cup of tea, with biscuits.'

So the attendant left with the full tray of food, leaving a pleasant smell of warm soup in her wake. Emanuel now truly became sad, but was forced to play out the comedy to the end.

'I'm feeling much better,' he mumbled.

'Rest quietly and you'll be fine, do you hear? I'm very sorry I can't stay,' she said, looking at her watch. 'I'm also very sorry you're suffering like this.'

A short bout of liver pain distorted Emanuel's face again, but he bore it admirably.

'It's not just this…' he murmured. 'All the distress, all the plaster is nothing compared to the horrific, frightening agony of being all alone in a room… every single day… every single day…'

Ernest finally understood and coughed approvingly.

'Why don't you come and see him more often?' Solange asked Ernest; Ernest said nothing while Emanuel continued moaning.

'Well then, I'll come and see you,' Solange said heroically. When? Solange thought for a moment. 'Sunday, for instance. On Sunday I am free all day…'

'Thank you… thank you so much,' moaned Emanuel in a final effort of humility and playacting.

'But please don't forget,' said Ernest.

They both made their way out. Left alone, Emanuel managed to relax for a while. The attendant came in with the tea.

'And the rest of it…' Emanuel ordered. 'You must bring the entire tray back… with all the food, everything… I'm hungry… I feel much better now.'

And he handed the anaemic, syrupy liquid back to the dumbfounded attendant.

That afternoon Emanuel could hardly complain of feeling abandoned. Many of the patients came to see him. Tonio was the first. He was in a downcast mood: a relative of Madame Wandeska had arrived a few days before, a so-called cousin, who was supposed to take her back home.

'What am I going to do all by myself?' he worried.

The enigma of this young cousin tormented him especially; he was pleasant-looking enough and could turn out to be, possibly, a lover…

Later Zed made a short visit on his trolley. Towards evening when Emanuel was once again alone, Quitonce came, the patient with the two canes who walked by flinging his legs around.

He stayed for a long time.

He was quite young, but his hair was graying at the temples. He seemed never to give a thought to his infirmity. But he confessed otherwise.

'You understand? I've been sick since I was a boy. I know all the doctors, all the nurses, all the sanatoriums of Europe… There are international crooks who have scoured the entire globe and know precisely what city, what company is ripe for a hit… Well, *I* know by heart the geography of bone disease clinics. I can tell you what sanatorium in Switzerland boasts the friendliest nurses and where in Germany you can get the best plaster… I am a specialist… In my career as a patient I have surpassed dilettantism. I have become a true professional.'

Quitonce was the son of a renowned engineer in Paris. Emanuel had once seen in a newspaper a photo of Quitonce senior at the inauguration of a celebrated feat of engineering.

'You are a hero of the disease, not a professional...' Emanuel told him.

'What does that mean – to be a hero?' Quitonce jumped in. 'If to be victorious in the world means that you are a hero, I haven't won anything and I'm not a hero. Let me tell you something about the heroism of patients...'

He paused to take a breath. He was somewhat asthmatic and this gave the conversation a great sense of calm and a great appeal. However, he kept his peaceful, even tone of voice only for as long as he sat on the chair. Whenever he stood, the jerking mechanism of his legs immediately went into action and the rest of his body quivered like a factory that begins throbbing the moment its powerful engines come to life.

'In order to become a hero, in order to achieve a target,' continued Quitonce with a slight tone of weariness in his voice, 'you need a certain energy and a certain willpower to overcome a great number of difficulties. Well, every invalid displays these. In the space of one year, an invalid expends exactly the same amount of energy and willpower one would need to conquer an empire... Except only that he consumes it in pure loss. That is why invalids could be called the most negative of heroes. Each one of us is "the one who wasn't Caesar", even though he has fulfilled all the conditions necessary for being one. Do you understand? To be possessed of all the component elements of a Caesar and yet to be... an invalid. It is a supremely ironic form of heroism.'

He ran his hand over his face as if it were a mask. He seemed somewhat preoccupied by something other than what he was talking about.

'Two weeks from now, or maybe a month, I don't know exactly when, they will operate on me again. It will be the twelfth operation of my life... They've removed rotten toes, bits of my skull. Look at the scars here... and there... and here... Well, if along with everything else I lacked the heroism to cope with this new test, I would commit suicide... I couldn't bear it...'

'And yet you will bear it,' said Emanuel.

'Certainly... certainly... But "beyond" heroism I have no courage... no hope... nothing. Regarding the operation I have the same absolutely neutral feeling as I have when I drink a glass of water... neither courage nor cowardice... I drink a glass of water, that's all.'

He ran his hand over his cheek once more and sat quietly with his face hidden in his palm. The room had become dark, as Emanuel did not want to turn on the light and disturb the enchantment of this budding friendship.

'I have tried everything in life,' Quitonce began again. 'I have tried the entire gamut, from heartaches to – I was going to say the pleasures of the flesh – to foolishness... Let's have some light in here!'

He pulled a thick wallet out of his pocket and rummaged through it.

'Take a look at them yourself.'

He handed Emanuel a stack of photographs.

They were all pornographic photographs, and of rather good

quality. Each one showed the same figure of a robust naked male, in full virile tension, flanked by the finely-shaped bodies of two women.

Emanuel, looking more closely at the photographs, realised that the hypersexual male was none other than Quitonce himself.

'I always regained my powers between operations,' he explained. 'What do you think? Provocative, aren't they?'

Emanuel was tortured by a question, which, however, he didn't ask. Did Quitonce fling his legs around him during sex the way he does when he walks? The vision of a clown unleashed, frenetically hurling his limbs around, his flesh quivering with amorous desire, was embarrassing. He handed the photographs back and thanked him.

'Provocative, eh?' repeated Quitonce, clicking his tongue.

That night Emanuel was tormented by terrible desires. It was a unique form of suffering, and horribly focused. His sex had become a living affliction, a sharp inner torture of the flesh itself, that ripped from his pubis, along with his exhausted virility, any remnants of the calm that is necessary for sleep. It was a supreme arousal stabbing deep into his flesh, a prisoner's pre-eminent struggle…

Then, toward morning, as the cast dried out inside, his skin began itching. It was a new torment, a new distress, a new cold, hallucinatory agony. In vain Emanuel ran his hands helplessly across the corset. His nails merely scratched the thick plaster tunic. Beneath the plaster, the surface of his skin caught fire in different places at random, and the irritation multiplied frenetically as if acid was percolating through the plaster, or a tiny claw was taking a stroll around the delicate meshwork of his nerves.

He closed his eyes and squeezed his eyelids tight, feeling that he could no longer withstand so much calm, demented irritation. He tried scratching himself, rubbing his skin against the walls of the plaster, but new territories of the skin ignited in a frenzy of itching, while at the same time his sexual urges grew ever more intense, in parallel with the prickling in his flesh.

With all his might, Emanuel concentrated every fibre of his face one more time in a huge effort of resistance.

With clenched fists, and eyelids squeezed as tight as possible, he steeled himself to await the consummation of the burning that had taken possession of his body.

9

FINALLY SUNDAY CAME. The rain had stopped. All the patients had been brought outside. They lay on their stretcher-beds in a neat row under a narrow awning made of dirty canvas, once yellow but now faded by rain. Opposite them the sanatorium building rose up, haunting and sombre. The whole garden consisted of a few pitiful metres of dry turf and a couple of withered rose bushes: a humble, sad garden, shut in by walls, like an animal suffering in a coop.

Emanuel was well wrapped up in two blankets to protect him from the cold gusts of wind. A humid breeze cut in from the ocean, carrying with it a powerful reek of algae and putrefaction.

He was impatiently waiting for Solange, even though he knew perfectly well that she was not going to come in the morning.

He lit a cigarette and puffed calmly as the smoke formed a tangled strand that was torn apart by the wind while Emanuel followed its progress, motionless, silent, devoid of thoughts.

His whole terrible night of agony and torment had evaporated amazingly in the open air of the autumn morning. A rinse with cold water in the washbasin in his room had refreshed him as if he had put a new skin on his face and hands. He had absurdly, uselessly, run the waterlogged sponge over the plaster tunic as well, as if to give himself a strictly moral kind of satisfaction. He had then put on his shirt properly as if over a clean body. The inside of the cast had dried almost completely.

Emanuel stayed in the garden, away from the other patients, until lunchtime. That afternoon he shut himself in his room in feverish anticipation.

An empty atmosphere of Sunday afternoon boredom reigned over the sanatorium. From time to time the crackly, disembodied echo of a gramophone record drifted from some room or other, before silence fell once again, even more profound and hypnotic. He pricked up his ears at the slightest noise in the corridor. Was it Solange this time? The steps would approach deceptively, then abruptly turn into the indifferent walk of a stranger, like a sleight-of-hand trick, where one object is quickly substituted for another.

He waited in vain for her till late in the evening.

Solange did not come that day, nor the next. In exasperation he sent an attendant to take a note to the boarding house where she lived, but this too brought no result. Humiliated, Emanuel smouldered with a controlled but violent hostility. The anticipation of seeing her turned into the desire never to see her again, but this desire was just as lucid and obsessive as the other. Another hour passed, another day, full of this anticipation of *not* seeing her. He knew that circumstances would bring them face-to-face once again and he calculated the probable length of time in which this meeting would *not* occur.

One evening towards the end of the week, Solange unexpectedly knocked on the door. 'What will she tell me?' thought Emanuel. 'What absurd and banal excuse will she invoke?' Solange came into the room out of breath and with cheeks aflame. Had she been running? Why was she in such a hurry? 'What a farce,' thought Emanuel. It had been four days since she had received his note, and she had had all the time in the world to get there at her leisure...

She held the note open in her hand. She was wearing a simple travel raincoat.

'Are you angry that I didn't reply straight away?' she asked, seeing his sulky look. Emanuel did not answer.

'I came directly from the train station. I only stopped at the boarding house for as long as it took to read your note. Look, the day I left here, my boss had important business to sort out in Paris and took me with him... There's a factory near here merging with some others. You can't imagine how many figures and paragraphs are stored away in these factory owners' paunches...'

She spoke quickly in order to pacify Emanuel, watching his face for signs of his cheering up.

'On Sunday I had two hours off. That's all. I bought a sandwich and went to see a film so I could entertain myself, have a rest and get something to eat, all in the same short space of time.'

Emanuel felt the dour indifference he had nursed towards her during the last few days instantly vaporise as if in an explosive flash. He would have liked to have clasped her hands there and then, and kissed them and told her he loved her so that this moment, so insipid and common to the beginning of all love stories, would be over more quickly.

Solange took off her raincoat.

Emanuel gazed at her, tall and simply dressed in front of him, and shivered slightly at her bewildering presence, total, inexpressible, and suddenly contained in the room which had been so horribly desolate before.

She sat down on the bed, next to him, the same way she had sat a few days before. A light-headed feeling of tangibility after his prolonged waiting...

During the trip her dress had become infected by the sour air of the train compartment, but behind this transparent smell Emanuel found again the familiar scent of lavender.

In the end he enquired if she wanted something to eat. She asked for an orange and a cup of tea.

He watched her in an unclouded reverie as she ate the orange. Every movement she made increased the simple abundance of their reunion. She had cut the orange into quarters, and she bit into the red and juicy flesh so deeply that tiny white strands of pith stuck between her teeth.

'Forgive me, I'm devouring the orange like a savage,' she apologised.

For the last few minutes Emanuel had felt overwhelmed by the encumbrance of the plaster cast. Specifically, since the moment when the thought passed through his mind that Solange might become his lover.

But to the same extent that the burden of the corset weighed him down, he was also tortured by Solange's clear, easy manner. He was searching for a few simple and direct words to say to her, but all his unspoken sentences faded quickly in the face of her simple and straightforward presence.

For a while they kept up a friendly conversation.

Solange told him about minor incidents from her trip and described her boss as a businessman whose 'basic goal in life must long have hovered indecisively between the temptation to become a butcher or a dogcatcher.'

Emanuel was tortured by the thought of taking her hand in his. Will she put up resistance? Will she draw it back? Solange's hand rested indifferently on the iron bedpost.

He was paralysed especially by the precision of his imagination: he envisaged their idyll already long consummated, he traced the specific habits of their love which had never yet happened, he had sudden recollections of things that had never yet occurred, vibrant, passionate episodes that stole his attention and wrapped the atmosphere of the present in the tranquillity of events long past...

Then all at once all thought stupidly became anchored in the impossibility of taking her hand; in the paralysis of the simplest and most immediate action. Finally, with a supreme effort, he succeeded in thrusting forth his hand, but this action was so abrupt and brutal that Solange fell silent, frightened.

Now he clutched her hand forcefully between his bony fingers, his eyes closed as if hypnotised in a magnetism experiment.

Solange looked at him, puzzled, but when Emanuel drew her toward him she understood and gave herself willingly to his lips, without a struggle and without any protest. Her mouth quivered slightly.

The scent of her hair seared Emanuel no less than the fascinating surprise of the kiss, and the limpid warmth of her uncovered arm.

'I know very well what I am doing,' she murmured. 'This is why I came.'

She wrapped him in her arms and glued her burning cheeks to his.

Then something dreadful happened. For a brief moment Emanuel had forgotten about the corset, but now, wrapped in Solange's arms, its weight bore down on him intolerably. Solange was embracing a bust of stone. In vain Emanuel slid his hands over her shoulders. Between them, the plaster became a barrier of indifference, a separate organism, impersonal and horribly hard... He almost cried from rage. The pitilessness of the corset whipped his blood up more fiercely and redoubled his desire. Deliriously, he stroked her arms, then her thighs. All at once he could feel the material of her dress, the top of her stockings, the smoothness of her skin.

He managed to extend his arm and turn off the light. In the total darkness everything rushed headlong with an increasingly impetuous passion, but which deteriorated into a helpless, tooth-gnashing struggle on the stretcher-bed.

Then, at the moment when Emanuel eased his hand beneath her dress and touched the warmth of her body, the ineffable burning angle where her thighs joined, Solange murmured:

'This isn't going to do you any good…'

Emanuel shuddered deep inside; his terrible light-headedness had only revived with the increasing arousal of his awakening desires. The whispered words seared through him like a boiling, corrosive liquid in his blood. 'This isn't going to do you any good!' he repeated, 'This!' That is, what he desired most, what inflamed him and stirred him up so perilously at that instant.

Now he touched her secret femininity and his suffering became almost furious.

In vain he tried to slide over to the bed; the corset kept him imprisoned, bound to the stretcher-bed. Solange lay down with her head next to his, alongside his body, encased in its corset like an inanimate mannequin.

Now, more than ever, the plaster was impeding the natural freedom of his movements…

Naked save for his corset, Emanuel was unable in his convulsions to penetrate anything except between her calves, between her close-pressed thighs, where her burning flesh deceived him for an instant… An instant in which his exaltation grew immense and unleashed itself in consummated exhaustion.

It was a vital and natural passion, reduced to an embarrassing simulacrum, that left Emanuel humiliated and ashamed.

He switched on the light in disgust. A bitter, draining desperation droned within his skull like an inexhaustible machine that could not be shut off.

Solange caressed his forehead, then, sensing all his distress, pressed her cheek again to his.

'Please don't be sad… Far rather than be in bed with you, I

should like to be the dog who sleeps in your doorway. It's all the devotion of which I feel capable...'

Emanuel sensed that a part of his life, unrestrained and essential, had gone from within him, perhaps permanently. A calm and painful bitterness took its place, like a new inner light, full of sorrow.

10

THAT WEEK SOMETHING took place that made a deep impression on Emanuel.

For several days Tonio had been out of sorts. He roamed the corridors in a state of confusion, his shirt undone, trailing his tie behind him like a dog leash. The day of Madame Wandeska's departure was approaching.

'Oh, if only I knew for sure that the blond beanpole who never leaves her sight is not her lover!' he told Ernest one evening.

In the dining hall he maintained his usual attitude of dignity and indifference. He walked in leaning on a single cane and lifted his head slightly as he acknowledged Madame Wandeska with a vaguely distracted glance.

He insisted upon bearing his misery with a cold and

manly pride. But in his eyes floated all the melancholy of his sleepless nights.

A single gesture might escape his control, or a small sign; sometimes a visible nuance appeared in the pallor of his face that could deceive no one.

And he tried, the poor lad, to limp as little as possible when he came in sight of the healthy cousin with the ruddy cheeks.

Whenever Emanuel went out in his carriage, he would find Tonio at a table in front of a third-class bar on the esplanade, his eyes vacant, behind a glass of yellow liquid which he sipped with a straw. It looked like orange juice, but it was something entirely different.

'It's an invention of the landlord here,' babbled Tonio, 'it's very good... brandy mixed with rum and a couple of egg yolks. Very good, and very fortifying...'

It was so fortifying that when he rose from the table he could hardly keep his balance. In vain did Ernest and Emanuel try to convince him that his suspicions were groundless.

One afternoon, drunker than usual, he couldn't control his disquiet. He came running to Ernest. He had got an idea into his head: 'Emanuel's room – it's right next to Madame Wandeska's, isn't it?'

'That's right,' replied Ernest.

'I saw a wardrobe in Emanuel's room that I'm sure is hiding a door behind it. What if tonight... you understand?'

Ernest pretended not to understand.

'Oh come on... don't you get it? I go there tonight when her cousin comes to visit, I push the wardrobe aside, I listen at the door and then I'll know for sure if...'

He couldn't bear to give voice to his dreadful supposition, to have to hear his own words.

'We'd need to ask Emanuel,' said Ernest, 'don't you think?'

They went to his room but did not find him. He had gone out to the beach in his carriage.

Tonio burned with impatience. The idea had got into his head and it spun there frenetically like a whirligig, shredding his mesh of thoughts like the strands of a cobweb.

Never mind that he had to wait till evening: he rushed to the beach to look for Emanuel as if his eagerness could speed up time, thrashing it to make it run faster. Huffing and puffing he climbed the hill that led to the ocean. Irritation, jealousy and drunkenness transmuted within him into a ferocious determination to find his friend.

It was a massive concentration of raw emotion upon a small and unimportant object, like a ridiculously excessive deployment of troops filling a narrow trench to overflowing.

He found the beach completely empty. As far as the eye could see the sand stretched out flat into the distance, as if the whole place had blatantly been emptied for the sake of exasperating him.

He wandered chaotically for a time on the water's edge, on the shore of that serene immensity, as if lost in the desert of his own personal distress. The sun was setting with the same stupid, useless display of grandeur that nature always puts on during a serious crisis.

He went back to the sanatorium and flung himself into an armchair in the main hall.

He sent a boy out to buy cigarettes.

'What kind of cigarettes?' asked the boy.

'Just get the cheapest,' replied Tonio.

For him it was a new kind of mortification.

He grabbed a newspaper, but the letters made fun of him capriciously, dissolving completely or coagulating in hard blocks, impassable barriers to him. He followed the passage of time on the enormous clock on the wall. The surface of the dial laboriously absorbed his impatience and filtered it, all too slowly, into precisely measured minutes.

He lit one cigarette, then another…

He was so absorbed in waiting, so intent upon his inner thoughts, that he failed to recognise Emanuel when his horse-drawn carriage crossed in front of the open window. For a few seconds this one simple thing for which he had been fervently waiting for two hours floundered around in his head like a puzzle. 'Emanuel went past… So what?'

Aha! He remembered that it was precisely him he needed to talk to.

He abruptly threw away his cigarette and ran like a madman into the courtyard in order to greet him.

Emanuel was not alone, however. He was accompanied by Solange.

Tonio was forced to wait a few minutes more until she left. They went into the sanatorium. He explained what he wanted with difficulty, his words in a jumble…

At that very moment, Madame Wandeska crossed the corridor in her stretcher-bed, being wheeled toward the dining hall by an attendant.

Tonio's gaze followed her the whole way. The cousin was with her, walking next to the carriage and reading a newspaper.

'Ah, the slut!' hissed Tonio, grinding his teeth.

He regretted it instantly.

'Please, I beg you to disregard what I said…'

He bit his lips a little in order to get his blood flowing once again.

That evening, straight after dinner, he came to Emanuel's room. He had exhausted himself during the day and was now forced to use his crutches. He slowly pushed the wardrobe aside, but when he had finished he seemed disappointed.

'Eavesdropping behind closed doors… Ah, no! Never!'

He left without even bidding Emanuel good evening, but after only a few steps down the corridor he came back. A painful silence fell in the room. Emanuel picked up a book, opened it doubtfully and immersed himself in it. The lift was bringing patients upstairs. They could hear its muted hum, and the pauses as it stopped at each floor.

Now the elevator opened on the third floor. It was Madame Wandeska; her trolley had a slight squeak which Emanuel recognised immediately. He could identify all the sounds in the sanatorium. He could tell without fail the vigilant footsteps of the attendants and the surreptitious tiptoe of the nurses… He recognised the ungreased wheels of each and every trolley. He could hear every single movement in the room next door…

'She's alone for the time being,' said Tonio.

He tried to lift his head to look Emanuel in the eye but quickly lowered his gaze… Emanuel turned off the light.

'Yes, that's better,' whispered Tonio. 'How contemptible, to be eavesdropping behind closed doors…'

'Shhh!… Quiet!' Emanuel interrupted.

Her attendant had come in. They could hear her slowly undressing Madame Wandeska and speaking to her in whispers. In the darkness each sound stood out, its contours clearly defined; now it was her dress falling onto a chair, then the rustle of her night-shirt, a book picked up from the table and put down somewhere closer… Then the girl left and all was quiet once more. Emanuel and Tonio waited silently in the dark. How long did they stay like this? A few minutes passed, perhaps more, perhaps half an hour.

Someone came to the door of Madame Wandeska's room. Their attention grew immense. Emanuel felt his pulse throbbing in his clenched fists.

'It's him,' murmured Tonio.

A discreet knock or two on the door, then someone went in. Some indistinct whispering could be heard.

'Yes, close the door…' Madame Wandeska said loudly, and the key turned in the lock.

Silence reigned once more.

There was whispering, impossible to make out. Footsteps could be heard in the room, walking from one place to another. From time to time Madame Wandeska laughed lightly. On the other side of the wall, in the darkness, drifted a sense of intense curiosity and furtive apprehension, as if the wall could at any moment turn transparent and the two of them be discovered listening at the door.

The more their anticipation increased, the more indistinct the noises became. The buzzing in their heads from their excruciating concentration drowned out the whispers from next door. Tonio put his hand on his heart; in order for him to hear better, he needed it not to beat so loudly…

Suddenly both of them stopped breathing.

There were tiny noises like kisses, as if skin were being touched by lips here and there, passionately, distractedly. Tonio's imagination went up in a blaze. He listened as all his anxieties came crowding into his skull; it was as if all his blood had rushed at once to his head. He felt his cheeks burning.

Yes, it was clear now. There… she made room for him next to her… more laughter… Tonio clenched his jaw. He wanted to cry, to run up and down the corridors, to scream. He thought of throwing himself down the elevator chute. But how? When?

In the darkness Emanuel felt the weight of a burning hand suddenly placed on his.

More rustling noises came from next door, a few jerky motions, then silence… bodies holding each other tight… tossing, moaning perhaps… Was it true? A louder noise startled them… Footsteps, then a cup of water suddenly poured into a basin. A real noise, shattering the tension.

'I'm going next door,' said Tonio distractedly, and stood up. Emanuel could not believe that he would really dare, but he heard the Argentinean picking up his crutches.

Fumbling with his arms outstretched Emanuel managed to grab one crutch but Tonio tried to snatch it away from him.

'Tonio, calm down, wait,' muttered Emanuel, not knowing what to say to quieten him.

There was no doubt about what they had heard from next door…

'I'm walking in on them,' whispered Tonio, as if hallucinating. 'To see them naked.'

He grabbed the crutch forcefully and took hold of it. Then he went out, leaving the door open.

The whole sanatorium was now completely silent except for Tonio's steps in the corridor.

He paused in front of the next door, listening attentively, the better to hear their final movements inside, and to imagine more precisely the obscene position in which he would find them.

Then he knocked violently on the door. In the silence the knocks resounded with a terrible echo.

'Who is it?' asked Madame Wandeska's frightened voice.

Emanuel anxiously awaited Tonio's answer, but Tonio seemed to have choked on the words; he could not manage to articulate them. He knocked again.

'Who is it? Who is it? What is this about…?'

'It's me, Tonio… I came by to say good night…'

'Oh! You gave me a terrible fright,' Madame Wandeska could be heard replying. 'Why so much noise? What's happened?'

'Open up,' Tonio nearly howled.

'Just one moment… one minute… wait.'

In the room next door there was a rush to put scattered things in order, then at once the key could be heard turning in the lock and the door opening.

A few moments of paralysing, tremulous impatience followed for Emanuel.

'Good evening… I came to say good evening.' He could now hear Tonio speaking in the room next door, but his voice was changed and confused, as if someone had knocked him hard on the head. Madame Wandeska was saying something to him...

Instead of the shouting match he had expected, Emanuel was listening now to a calm, whispered conversation.

Soon Tonio left the room and returned. Emanuel turned on the light. The Argentinean's face was frighteningly changed. He was exhausted, drained, his crutches dragging like a pair of broken wings.

He regarded Emanuel as if he had just awakened from sleep.

'What happened?'

But Tonio was unable to speak.

At last he muttered: 'The nurse was there... she was giving her the weekly bath... like the rest of the patients... those were the noises we heard... the water pouring... Everything we took to be... was nothing but that... washing... the water splashing when she was being washed... by the nurse...'

He stood staring at nothing, confused and terribly ashamed. Suddenly, with incredible violence considering the flabby and exhausted condition of his body, he began striking himself on the head with his crutch, harder and harder.

'What a bastard I am,' he muttered. 'What a bastard.'

11

EMANUEL WENT OUT in his carriage more often now, accompanied by Solange. She would try to finish her work in the morning in order to have the afternoons free. The dreadful autumn weather had begun, with its constant drizzle that covered the streets with a fine weft, with its subterranean grey light, with its ragged winds gusting through the deserted town, on blustery and infinitely fragile afternoons... The beach was empty. The ocean lapped it with feeble waves that foamed unpleasantly yellow. They went out more often into the countryside, by narrow and abandoned roads through dunes covered in winter vegetation, enormous grasses sticking out of the sand like swords and endless stretches of dried-up thorns like real wounds, brown and blue, upon the earth.

From time to time they were caught in the rain; although

they put the carriage's top up, the water came in in bursts and splashed their cheeks. Solange wiped Emanuel's face while he drove the horse on. They found refuge by the side of the road, near the high wall of a country estate. There, sheltered from the storm and the whole world, they embraced without enthusiasm, their cheeks still damp from the rain. Solange jumped from the carriage and picked weeds from the field that carried a brisk, wild scent of earth, or leaves that reeked faintly of corpses when they rubbed them insistently between their fingers. She covered the whole carriage with brambles and dressed the top with the immense leaves of wild plants, grief-green and sombre. They returned looking like gypsies, their caravan resplendent with wild vegetation.

Many times they stopped at country inns with ruddy-cheeked landladies solemnly dressed in black lace, as if in their Sunday best. There they ate meats still dripping with the fresh taste of blood and were given to drink a black and bitter peasant beer still heavy with the hops from which it was made. It was the most delicious drink Emanuel had ever tasted.

Once they found themselves at an inn lost among bushes and brambles where they asked for coffee with milk; it was served steaming hot in two large soup plates, on a tray with spoons on the side. Emanuel was somewhat taken aback by this manner of serving it.

'This is how we have our coffee around here,' said the proprietor, a peasant every bit as wild and unsophisticated as the deserted place where the inn was located. 'We like to put bits of bread in it, too...'

He brought two slices of rough bread which Emanuel and Solange broke into bits and dipped into their coffee bowls.

Autumn cloaked them with a cloudy sky, like the ceiling of an immense hall in which no one but them had ever existed. Their hands were blue with cold, the wind blew in biting gusts. It was an idyll filled with stark, primitive realities.

At times Emanuel's hands froze on the reins. He would stop to shake his fingers and loosen the cramp that held them constricted for hours. Solange would take them and place them under her jersey, under her blouse, pressing them close to her hot flesh, her burning breasts. They were like two blocks of ice placed on her skin, but she closed her eyes and suffered the cold while his hands slowly came back to life.

Her warmth insinuated itself into him in fine strands like water trickling through his fingers into the whole of his body. They communicated with each other in this way, through blood and heat, deep into the dark heart of their being. This contact between them unified the circulation in their veins, and Emanuel found his own pulse repeated in the beating of her heart.

He would draw her towards him and kiss her hair. He would lean his head on her shoulder and breathe in her warm, womanly scent of lavender. She was an animal every bit as splendid as his horse, which he adored more than anything, and he would tell her:

'You are as beautiful as Blanchette…'

The mare, hearing her name, would turn her head. She was a pure-bred from Normandy with tufts of thick hair about her hooves and a short mane rough as a brush. From where he lay

Emanuel could see only her powerful haunches but he would call her name and she would turn her head, gazing at him with the large melancholy eyes of a bored human asking for a cigarette (and it was a pity he did not smoke, as it would have been so natural for a horse to hold a pipe between its teeth). Emanuel would send her lumps of sugar via Solange and Blanchette would take them in her wide black lips, sniffing at her outstretched palm.

'You are as beautiful as she is… Your haunches are as broad and handsome as hers,' he would tell Solange. Then he would slide his hand under her dress and caress her calves, her hot thighs and her broad back, the hollow of her back, then, lower down, the fullness of her young mare's haunches.

'And who do you love more?' asked Solange.

'I love you both the same…'

'And we do too,' replied Solange, accentuating that 'we' which joined her in animal fellowship with Blanchette.

Emanuel pulled her next to him on the stretcher-bed and held her close, after which he would roll over and crush her beneath the weight of his body and the plaster. By now he was used to his corset and was able to move in ways which he would never have suspected possible. Solange moaned gently from pleasure and because of the weight pressing down on her. In certain places the plaster would penetrate between her thighs and she would feel pain mingled with the ecstasy of their passion, like a bitter realisation of the severity of their love, consummated in the immense open air of the dunes, surrounded by unbounded wilderness.

Then Emanuel returned to his reclining position, spent with exhaustion, eyes wide open and lost in an impenetrable white sky that became the exact counterpart of the sense of inner stillness that came with those minutes.

It was a blissfulness with an astringent taste, plain, slightly brutal, like Solange herself.

Those were their days of roaming through the dunes. In the course of some afternoons the skies would brighten and the clouds become golden tracery, like enormous objects dug up from the earth that still held a gilded brilliance about the edges of their reliefwork. Emanuel drove the horse toward a hidden place, over a little raised bridge, by an inlet where the sunset glowed in the infinite shades of a bloody cataclysm.

In this inlet the retreating ocean left in its wake thousands of miniature trenches filled with water, dug deep into the sand.

The dying sun set them aflame with red until the whole stretch of sand became a weft of blood and fire. It was as if the earth had been flayed alive in that place, so as to lay bare its most intimate veins, its arteries, burning and terrible, streaming with gold and purple fire. It was a moment of frightening grandeur that took their breath away.

The sun slowly sank behind the horizon, shedding its last streams of blood. The whole sky darkened suddenly, like the thickening of a chemical solution, and within its deep blue, the radiant weft assumed the subtlety and precision of a construction made of steel, an enormous, bizarre, metallic design stretching far into the distance.

Emanuel and Solange left the place, their souls exhausted with beauty.

12

ONE EVENING AROUND the beginning of December, Emanuel received a note from Quitonce inviting him to his room. It was the eve of his operation and he wanted to see him one more time to bid him farewell. This liturgy of goodwill and friendship prevailed in the sanatorium on the day preceding any critical event.

He found Quitonce on his bed looking a little pale, wrapped up to his neck in white gauze.

'They've washed me, they've shaved my whole body, they've anointed me with iodine and shrouded me in bandages like a mummy,' said Quitonce. 'Look at me. I've been prepared for my eventual role as a corpse...'

'Hush, don't speak like that,' Eva reproved him.

She was bustling around the room, looking for things to do,

lining up the books on the shelves, wiping away an imaginary speck of dust, as if the room needed to be made ready to undergo an operation of its own.

Before she left the room, she once again approached Quitonce's bed: 'Are you feeling well? Are you hungry? Thirsty?'

'I think I'm more hungry than thirsty…' replied Quitonce, who had been fasting that day. 'Why are you still asking?' he barked. He was exhausted by all the preparations before the operation, all the tests that had to be done, but above all by the anxious, funereal expressions of the doctor and nurses. As soon as Eva left the room, he let out a sigh of relief. He sat up on his pillows, supporting himself on his elbows:

'All this warm love that she shows me is not without its purpose… Eva wants me to will her my gramophone; she's got her eyes on it… I tell you, she couldn't care less if I'm hungry or thirsty, or if I have a headache. She is set on the gramophone and exhausts herself in useless devotions. It's a well-known trick…'

Quitonce was suppressing a dispassionate inner anxiety. His nervousness ran like an electric current through the tips of his fingers, which were trembling slightly.

'It's impossible to have reliable dealings with fate,' he said, changing the tone and subject of the conversation. 'Ever since last night I have been desperately trying to find out what are the chances of my survival tomorrow.'

He picked up a dictionary from the bedside table and opened it at random. '1,257,' he read at the top of the page. Then he began to add the numbers. 'One plus two is three… plus five makes eight… plus seven, fifteen… that is, five: undecided. I'd like to get

more than five, or less than five, three times in a row… but anyway
I'd like to know for certain what my fate is: live or die? Ever since
last night, I keep getting the same kind of result… six… four…
then five again… It's a terrible thing when fate is vacillating within
such a short range… It's as if it was shuddering …

'In fact,' he began again, 'it's theoretically impossible to get
a true and exact prediction… Even if these predictions could be
exact, try to imagine how many Quitonces like me are waiting
this evening for an operation tomorrow. How many invalids like
me might there be in the world, trying their best to divine the
verdict in advance? Diffused among so many people, any prophecy
becomes imprecise… A prediction that's been diluted so much
becomes watery…'

The room was quiet and a little cold. The door to the terrace
had been left open and the cool of the night came in from outside
as if in the wake of the beating of a gigantic wing. For a while they
remained silent. Then suddenly Quitonce furrowed his brow, as he
peered into the darkness, and began laughing quietly, apparently
to himself; he picked up the dictionary, and began to read out the
definitions in a loud voice.

Emanuel did not understand what was going on. Quitonce
could not stop laughing as he read out all sorts of absurdities. After
a few minutes he looked outside again and closed the dictionary
with an air of satisfaction.

'There… Oh, good! She's gone now! Did you think I'd gone
mad? You see over there, a rectangular patch of light?'

He pointed to the exact place in the darkness.

'It's the reflection of our open door in the windows of the

terrace,' he went on. 'I suddenly noticed a shadow gliding along. Someone came from outside to listen to what we were saying...'

He was extremely amused by his discovery.

'It was Eva, the nurse... always Eva... who wanted to eavesdrop, make sure I hadn't somehow got you here to sell you the gramophone. I started reading from the dictionary to give her her fill of espionage... She probably can't sleep at night, worrying about the gramophone!'

He then explained the next day's operation in detail: it was a matter of removing a tumour that had grown in one of the vertebrae; the tumour was pressing upon the marrow of his spine, causing all the disorder in his legs when he walked.

The operation was extremely delicate... it had to be performed with infinite precaution in order not to injure the marrow, and thus potentially cause more serious disturbance to the spine.

Emanuel decided that staying longer would run the risk of tiring Quitonce, so he asked him to ring for an attendant.

At that very moment a short elderly gentleman with a white goatee and gold wire-rimmed glasses entered the room.

'I forgot to tell you my parents are here because of the operation. Stay a few more minutes,' said Quitonce.

His mother came in too, a dignified elderly lady, her white hair combed into a tall pompadour like a wig. The engineer inquired after Emanuel's illness.

He encouraged him with gentle, sympathetic words, then began talking about his boy.

'He, too, will soon be well,' he said, pointing to his son on the bed. 'Yes... Yes, I am sure... All my life I have been successful... in everything I have undertaken… I have dared do things that no one believed in. I have built bridges that my students doff their hats to, when they go across. Yes… They take off their hats… But you see, when it comes to my son's vertebrae, things have run aground a little… But he will survive! We'll all meet one year from now in Paris, in the most elegant restaurant. We'll have a fantastic feast. Papa Quitonce will pay for everything…'

The old man's optimism was lost in the silence of the room like machinery whirring in a vacuum.

Quitonce's mother, fretful and grim-faced, paced the room, listening to the conversation and pausing from time to time before the bookcase, reading the titles of books with the strained attention of someone so eaten by worry that they see nothing of what is in front of their eyes…

Early next morning Emanuel went out to the beach in his carriage. The sky had become clear, turning an intense, almost stern, shade of blue. It was a calm and sunny December day.

In the distance the ocean's limitless surface sparkled like platinum. With all their windows lit up in gold by the sun, the line of villas on the esplanade looked like miniature buildings, a child's toys.

A few sailors came from the direction of the town and immediately went about their work. The tide was high and they were starting to drag their boats into the water to launch them for fishing.

'Heer! Uuup!' they heaved in long, rhythmic shouts, straining on the ropes tied to the enormous sailing boats. The work was horrendously tough. The boats slid over the sand with great difficulty; the men's muscles strained, ready to burst.

'Heeer! Uuup!' they cried, and behind them the ships' hulls left deep furrows in the sand as if it had been cut by a plough.

Alone in his horse-drawn carriage, Emanuel wandered along the beach.

'I wonder what he is doing at this very moment?' It was the hour, of course, when Quitonce was being operated on. 'This very moment when I am free, here, gazing at the sea… Is some scalpel cutting deep into his flesh?'

Suddenly he felt the perfect futility of that splendid day.

In that moment, while the morning rose up, immense in its freshness, a sick man lay on an operating table somewhere as rivulets of blood leaked from him. The absurd, grotesque disparity of it all!

What infinite quantities of useless serenity the ocean held that morning, in the face of the fear and torment of a single man!

Emanuel eventually realised that he had driven the horse too far. The tide was rising continuously; he needed to turn back right away if he was to avoid being overtaken by the waves. He reached the esplanade around ten o'clock. He watered his horse from the stone fountain. While he lay back absentmindedly, watching Blanchette greedily drawing up water, he turned his head and spotted Quitonce's parents coming towards him, holding hands as if out for a stroll.

Was the operation over so quickly? Emanuel waved to them and sketched a smile. In any case, the thought that everything was over was easier to bear than the interminable anguish of waiting. His smile met only with disconsolation on the faces of the old couple.

'Is it over?' asked Emanuel. 'What do the doctors say? How is he feeling?'

'They're operating on him right now,' replied the engineer, staring at the tips of his fingers as if hypnotised.

Emanuel was bewildered.

'I thought that… after all… well, I didn't know,' he mumbled incoherently.

Meanwhile the old lady took her husband's arm once again.

'Come on, Quitonce…' she said.

It was a French custom that Emanuel had often noticed and been rather touched by, the almost humble deference which elderly ladies showed their husbands by addressing them like strangers by their family name: 'Come on, Quitonce…'

They continued down the esplanade with small steps and tired, wary eyes.

Back at the clinic Emanuel tried to find out about Quitonce from the nurses and attendants, but in vain. It was always the same stereotypical answer:

'He's fine… he's very well.' It was a kind of code used to desensitise the patients, a colourless, comfortable formula with which to withhold unpleasant information.

A few days passed without any definitive news. Emanuel passed Quitonce's room in the mornings when he was wheeled to the dining hall. A thick carpet had been laid on the floor in front of the room in order to deaden the noise in the corridor, while in the room absolute silence reigned and not a sound came from within.

One afternoon the engineer came to tell Emanuel that he might visit his son, as he was feeling better. It was growing dark. As Emanuel entered Quitonce's room he was unable to distinguish much at first. In the entire room only a single lamp was lit, next to the bed, which was covered with a thick blue blanket; the stuffy air smelled of iodoform and, possibly, valerian: a mixture of antiseptic and the slightly sickly smell of narcotics.

In the uncertain, dim light Emanuel could make out Quitonce's drawn yellow face; his head, sunk deep into the pillows, was that of an old man. The lamp's weak glow cast dull, greenish shadows on his face, giving it in places a translucent appearance.

He was alone in the room and had been waiting for Emanuel.

'How are you?' he murmured weakly, forcing out each word.

Emanuel lacked the courage to answer 'fine' or ask in turn how he was feeling; he said nothing.

'As far as I'm concerned,' Quitonce continued with painful difficulty, 'I think I'm on my way out... I might survive, maybe... if only... they would... give me... more... more injections a day... camphor oil shots, that's what I need... but they won't... they're all... all... all of them... pigs, yes... pigs... pigs...'

His asthma was affecting his breathing more than usual and from time to time he would cough, a short, dry, hacking noise that came from his chest like the rattling of some broken object. He would fasten onto a word and repeat it obsessively, distracted by it, until he suddenly recalled the rest of what he wanted to say.

Emanuel was about to reply when Eva entered with a syringe in her hand. She had come for his camphor oil shot; this happened twice a day, and though Quitonce would never have been able to handle more than that, he was nonetheless obsessed with the idea that it was not enough.

Nothing could convince him otherwise.

'It won't take a minute… don't go…'

In order to see better, the nurse removed the veil from the lamp. Suddenly the room brightened and its disarray and grime became fully apparent. The floor was scattered with wads of cotton and crumpled paper, while on the table medicine bottles were all mixed up with boxes and powders of various types.

The nurse removed the blankets and in the bare light a naked Quitonce appeared, wrapped in bandages, his body horribly thin; his face, which just before, in the darkness, had seemed covered in shadows, was filthy and unshaven.

At the centre of his nakedness, his shrivelled, purple sex hid itself under skin disfigured by large, yellow stains, burnt by iodine. It was the same sex that Emanuel had seen in the photographs in all the splendour of Quitonce's virility, and nothing was more disturbing than superimposing that mental image of him over the impoverished, miserable present reality.

Emanuel stared in shock at that shamefaced and cringing sex, that shrivelled, useless manhood, offering as it did a frightening sense of life's futility… It was a detail more human and more forceful than all the bandages and the agony of the operation itself. It was in itself an irrefutable indication of the paltry worth, in any case, of a man's body …

'In any case… in any case…' Emanuel repeated to himself, 'what can a man do with his body?' The revelation of affliction and suffering was made shockingly complete by this plain, humble evidence that demonstrated all at once both the exhaustion of the most essential part of life and the cold, disheartening invasion of pain even to the extremity of the body's endurance; to the point where Quitonce, from being a man of virile appetites and enthusiasms, became merely a congeries of progressively putrefying organs, with decomposing vertebrae and with a sex – the sex that once gave his body all its significance and vivacity – that was now a flaccid piece of meat mouldering slowly in advance of its ultimate putrefaction.

The nurse inserted the needle into the thigh and the skin swelled, soft and pallid, having no blood beneath it. When she was done, she inspected the bandage and put a gauze compress in one place to cover it better.

'Do you think there was any need for the gauze?' asked Quitonce as soon as Eva had left. 'She comes round like that to check on imaginary things… just to show me how devoted she is… oh, that gramophone…'

Emanuel was wanting to leave but Quitonce lifted his head from the pillows as if to say something important. 'I should like to give you something to remember me by… for you to keep as a memento… from Quitonce…'

With his emaciated hand he rummaged through his drawer and took out a small package wrapped in paper.

'I thought first of the photographs, you know the ones… but told myself it would be too painful to stare at a man doing dirty things… in a photograph… when you know he's lying in a grave…'

His cough was making his breathing more difficult, a result

perhaps of fatigue, perhaps of emotion. He handed the bit of paper to Emanuel, who unwrapped it.

What could such a small parcel contain? Was it a wood shaving, was it a tiny rock?

'It's a bit of bone from my vertebra,' explained Quitonce.

'I asked the surgeon's assistant to save it for me… You can take it in your hand… don't be afraid… it's been disinfected… it's been washed and washed again, in alcohol… Think about me when you look at it…'

Emanuel was too overwhelmed to answer; his temples throbbed and had the attendant not arrived at that moment to wheel him out, he might have passed out in that room, with its stink of valerian.

A few days later he met Quitonce's father in the garden. He had come by himself, to give him news.

'He's better…' he said. 'Much better… This morning he shaved himself… a good sign, the doctor said. Maybe in a week he will be coming down again to the dining room,' the old man added, with obvious happiness in his voice.

13

QUITONCE DIED TWO days before Christmas, in a bout of uproarious laughter. The illness mocked him till the end. His death-throes were marked by bursts of hilarity in the way other people's are usually filled with howls and moans. But how else could Quitonce die, who went hurling his legs around like a clown his entire life, other than in a fit of convulsive and grotesque laughter?

It was such a horrific laughter that its peals could be heard at night even in Emanuel's room. Their lugubrious, broken echo resounded through the sanatorium like the howling of an animal, culminating in unnerving shrieks. Truly the laughter of a tormented clown, a bitter hilarity that brought an agonising constriction of the heart.

Emanuel asked the doctor about this the next day.

'Sometimes the pain can be wrong about itself,' Dr. Cériez explained. 'Instead of switching on a cry of pain, it switches on a current of hilarity, travelling along the same nerve wires... You could say an invisible hand hits the wrong switch... It's the same current flowing, but it ends up being converted into a peal of laughter instead of a grimace of pain...'

The burial took place with the customary discretion always accorded such events at the sanatorium. At dawn a truck left, carrying the corpse to the town cemetery. Quitonce was buried at Berck according to his written wishes.

That morning, when Emanuel went in his trolley past the dead man's room, the door was already sealed with strips of paper in order to protect the corridor from the sulphur vapours that were used for disinfection. These were always sure signs of an operation or a death in the sanatorium. A thick carpet would appear in the corridor leading from the clinic for a few days, in order to deaden any sound, meaning that a patient had been operated on and was lying in one of the rooms there; then, after a few days, the carpet would be gone and the door cracks would be covered with newspaper. That was the sign that the patient was dead. Apart from this, nothing was said, there was no sound of lamentation, and the corpse was dispatched overnight so that the business could be dealt with more discreetly.

In the case of Quitonce, for example, who had not frequented the dining room for a month, no one in the sanatorium except for Ernest and Emanuel was aware that he had died. Everyone interpreted his prolonged absence in a completely normal fashion, supposing that he had moved to another clinic.

The day of the burial was sombre, laid waste by the wind and rain. Falling snowflakes mixed with the rainwater, forming a thin layer of mud in which all things seemed to splatter, even the air, even the spoken word...

Staring out at the garden from his window, Emanuel could see Quitonce's terrace perfectly. All his things were laid out in the open to be aired. Eva, evidently infuriated, had set them out with brutal carelessness.

Ernest came to visit at about four. He had bags under his eyes from lack of sleep and seemed exhausted. He had kept a vigil at Quitonce's bedside for two nights and then, that dawn, had accompanied the coffin to the cemetery. He looked out of the window and spotted a fuming and disgusted Eva clutching a mattress:.

'She's totally furious,' he muttered. 'Quitonce made a fool of her. He left it in writing that his gramophone should go to the children's dormitory, for them to have something to entertain them...'

At that moment, the mighty strains of a military march, played on the gramophone, came crashing from the children's terrace. The nurse cast a contemptuous look in that direction and threw the mattress she was holding onto the ground. Possibly she even swore.

'She's yellow with spite,' remarked Emanuel.

Ernest related a few details from the funeral. It had rained ceaselessly and the grave was half-filled with water. The coffin had been open as it was lowered into the hole; the corpse, plunging into the mire, sank almost completely in the mud. In vain had Quitonce taken care while still alive to keep a beautiful black suit at the ready in his wardrobe, just for this last occasion. The suit had become sopping wet and covered in mud.

'And then someone, I don't remember who, I think it was his father, threw a bouquet of flowers into the grave,' Ernest added. 'And the bouquet stayed floating on top of the puddle.'

Emanuel covered his eyes with his hand and sank into the pillows. This last image of Quitonce persisted in his mind like an absolute reality, but one that was distant now, and sadly unapproachable.

Winter at Berck brought with it a stormy wind from the north, with rain cascading as if waterfalls had been unleashed. Often a foggy thaw would leak upon the town, covering everything in grime.

At times the sky turned coal-black, then dissolved into cloud masses of lustreless grey, like a dripping swamp above the houses.

On Christmas Eve there was a celebration for the sanatorium's children. Solange arrived wearing a black dress that made her figure even taller and more elegant. In the hall stood an enormous fir tree covered with toys and lighted candles. The hubbub was so overwhelming that it was impossible to hear anything; the stretcher-beds were crammed into a corner and the children were cheering and shouting at the top of their voices. There was one little boy who had received a drum as a gift; after he had had enough of beating that, he unbuttoned his shirt and began drumming with his sticks on his plaster corset. The tree in the middle of the room gave off a suffocating smoke and the reek of burnt resin. All the children joined together in singing an old carol, laden with nostalgia.

Ernest came to toast a glass of wine with Emanuel and Solange.

'It's the sixth Christmas I've spent in the sanatorium,' he said.

'It's only my first,' replied Emanuel sadly.

That evening the patients were taken to church for midnight mass. Solange insisted on wheeling Emanuel's stretcher-bed herself. The night walk in the rain was good for him; it had been a long time since he had seen the streets of a town in the rain at night. The asphalt glimmered like stretched-out skin; over it the streetlamps poured down quivering tresses of pale electricity.

The interior of the church seemed to be dazzling with light, but only for that first moment when they came in from outside. It was a humble church, built by seamen out of beams and poles, exactly like a sailing ship. What would happen, thought Emanuel, if that evening the entire construction were to set out into the world like a ship, sailing the ocean waves, laden with patients, gleaming with light on its final nocturnal journey before the shipwreck, and then drowning along with itself all the plaster, all the infirmities and all the despair that was gathered together in that one place?

The patients lay on their trolleys, lined up in a long row; the priest stopped before each one of them, like a hospital doctor doing his rounds.

The wind blew chaotically through the beams, making the candle flames flicker during the service. Although they were well wrapped up, the patients were freezing almost to death.

When they returned, Emanuel invited Ernest and Solange to his room. They opened a bottle of wine, and Ernest raised his glass.

'To the health of the healthy,' he said cheerfully.

'What about the sick?' asked Solange.

'The sick have no need of health,' continued Ernest with the same spirit. 'They feel wonderful on their beds, the way they lie there all stretched out, wheeled all over the place, going out for drives in their carriage... happy indeed, entirely happy...'

'You think?' Emanuel asked sceptically.

'Certainly,' replied Ernest. 'My situation is far more tragic. As I have been cured, I'll soon have to rejoin everyday life. I will have to be healthy all the time, whereas on my stretcher-bed I can have a fever one night and throw up the next, just as I please...'

He downed nearly a whole glass of wine and became talkative.

'What could I actually do in daily life? What kind of amazing or extraordinary thing can there be in it for me? I will brush my teeth each day, I will have lunch, each evening I will drink my coffee with milk, no matter whether or not in the course of the day there has been a train crash somewhere, or someone in the family has died. I will still brush my teeth, I will still sit down to eat... I will still be me. Do you understand? Do you understand what a dreadfully monotonous animal I will become?'

He was silent for a moment, then continued.

'When someone is, all of a sudden, removed from life and has the time and the necessary calm to ask himself a single, essential question regarding it – one single question – he is poisoned forever... Yes, of course the world continues to exist, but someone has wiped away its significance with a sponge...'

Emanuel was no longer paying full attention. For several minutes he had been preoccupied with a small accident that had happened to him. When he brought the glass to his lips, in a moment of carelessness he had spilled part of its contents which had run down his neck and shoulders and right inside the cast. His whole back became wet and Emanuel tried by twisting his hand to insert it beneath the cast in order to pull his flannel shirt away from his skin. When he finally succeeded, he became aware of something very unpleasant: his hand reeked of mildew. In this way Emanuel discovered all at once the dirt and grime that had coated his unwashed body for several months. It was the first time he had explored under his corset. Suddenly he felt incredibly disgusted with himself and, the more he attempted to conceal his distress, the more obvious became the unhappiness on his face.

Ernest, believing that Emanuel had been upset by his words, wore the satisfied smile of a professor of dialectics who is winning his argument, and poured himself another glass of wine.

14

A NEW PATIENT took the place of Madame Wandeska at the dinner table. Ernest knew her: she had been living at Berck in a villa on the esplanade for many years with no one but a governess who took care of her. Now her illness had worsened and, needing to be bandaged everyday, she had moved to the clinic, where there were nurses at her disposal.

An air of mystery and eccentricity surrounded her. Speaking of her in the garden, someone had related how she had once taken a plane to Belgium, ill as she was, lying on her stretcher-bed. One day Emanuel ran into Cora, who was all dressed up and very excited.

'I am going to visit Isa,' she said. 'She's giving a reception today.'

Isa was the newly arrived patient at the sanatorium.

Emanuel could not mistake her when he saw her for the first

time in the dining hall. Her subtly refined clothes and gestures gave her an air of utmost simplicity.

He was especially intrigued by her unusual features: pronounced cheekbones that gave her a vaguely Mongolian air, and hair hanging along her forehead in a fringe, cut short in the manner of Chinese women (later he learned that she had been born in a colony in south Asia and that her mother was of mixed blood). Her complexion was pale, but in no way anaemic, reminiscent of the matte sheen of a highly polished, yellowish stone.

Ernest walked in and headed straight in her direction.

'May I introduce you to a friend?' he asked her after they exchanged a few words.

He pointed to Emanuel, at a table not too far away.

Isa twisted her mirror toward him and smiled, giving him a friendly wave of the hand.

That same evening at supper Emanuel found a book placed under his napkin, which she had sent along with a little note:

'Do you like reading? Do you know this book?'

It was a thick volume, bound in red morocco leather. Emanuel was a little flattered by this unexpected attention. He opened it and read at random:

'*…There, in a grove surrounded by flowers, deep in sleep, the hermaphrodite lies on grass wet with his tears. All around him the awakened birds, bewitched, contemplate his melancholy visage, while the nightingale has ceased to sing her crystal cavatinas… The forest has become solemn as a tomb…*'

Elsewhere, someone had underscored with a deep fingernail mark the words '… my eyes tormented by life's eternal sleeplessness.'

'Life's eternal sleeplessness...' Who was this strange author whose sadness revealed itself so profoundly and so movingly?

Emanuel looked at the title page: 'Comte de Lautréamont', and underneath, in thick letters: *Les Chants de Maldoror*.

He stayed up all night reading this astounding book. Dawn overtook him feverishly turning the pages, enchanted by their bewitching melancholy, tortured by their bitter imprecations, by their sublime abjection, by their poetic hallucination. This book encompassed everything that ennui, sadness, dream and frenzy could summon up in poems of fantastic and unsettling beauty.

In vain he cast around for anything comparable in what he had read before: this book resembled neither poetry, nor poetic sentimentality, nor crisis of literature. It contained a venomous fluid, that slowly, slowly, page by page, worked its way into the bloodstream, bringing dizziness and delirium, like an imperceptible but virulent infection.

He returned the volume the next day with a note asking when he might visit. He desired a better acquaintance with this girl with her sidelong glances and air of mystery, who instantly knew how to captivate him with such fascinating reading.

He received a reply that he could come to her room that very afternoon.

The nurse was waiting for him in the corridor at the appointed hour. Upon entering the room Emanuel was struck by a warm and pleasant smell of tea and fresh baking. The room looked like nothing else at the sanatorium. Though the white walls were no different, they had been covered in very dark red fabric. It gave the room a faintly oppressive, almost funerary atmosphere.

'I detest the sanitary white of the clinic… In those milk-white sanatorium rooms, I think one could do nothing more obvious or more fitting than go mad,' Isa explained as soon as they had greeted each other.

In the whole room there was not a single decoration. One enormous crystal vase sitting on top of a little wardrobe was filled with dry fir cones.

Expressing his thanks for the book, Emanuel wondered why there wasn't a bookcase to be seen in her room, or even a single volume.

'Oh, I don't like books! A book is nothing, it is not an object,' said Isa. 'It's a dead thing… that contains living things… it's like a putrefying corpse crawling with thousands upon thousands of insects. I keep all my books next door in my nurse's room, in a box under the bed.'

And she added in a whisper, like a confession:

'I'm ashamed of the fact that I can know life only from books…'

She called her nurse in order to introduce her. She was a hunchbacked old lady, with a face the colour of stale bread.

'This is Celina,' she said. 'Look at her and tell me she doesn't look like a beetle – a maybug. Except she doesn't buzz…'

The nurse was indeed cloaked in a tiny coffee-coloured cape, shining like an insect's elytra. She held her hands over her belly and was constantly rubbing one over the other, like a fly washing itself. She laughed a little at Isa's words, in short, careful jerks, as though she was mentally measuring out the quantity of joy an old lady of her sort could decently display.

'See how huddled up she is?' said Isa when Celina went out to fetch the tea. 'It's the moral reflex of modesty… Celina is the least of beings as regards her own needs and the most devoted when it comes to the whims of someone else…'

The tea was placed, steaming, on a little table between Isa and Emanuel.

'It's been a long time since I felt such intimacy,' he said. 'There is a calmness and peace in this room that I had almost forgotten. It's as if I have only now become aware, in my room here at the sanatorium, of the loneliness and alienation of the life I have been leading till today…'

'I have lived for years in that state of alienation, in rooms that don't belong to me and places quite foreign to those of my childhood,' said Isa, a little sadly. 'I got used to it, though, the same way I got used to my illness, to my cast… to the bandages… to all of it…'

Isa couldn't lift her head, so she sipped her tea from a cup fitted with a long spout like a teapot.

A friendly intimacy quickly established itself between them.

'I hugely admire those for whom illness is a matter of indifference,' said Emanuel. 'On the other hand, I would feel infinitely unhappier if one day I could reach such perfect resignation. I wake up sometimes in the middle of the night and finger my cast like a madman… Is it true? Is it really true? And I clench my jaw as my fingers slide along its hard surface, impotently…'

Isa became thoughtful for a moment.

'Do you think I didn't feel the same to start with, too?' she said. 'We have all been upset… We have all woken up in the depths of night and fingered our casts in desperation. All of us… all of us… but then, as the blows intensified, we no longer felt anything…

'Do you know the medical term "cicatrisation?" It's when scar tissue forms: that dark-coloured and wrinkled skin that forms on a wound as it heals. It's almost normal skin, except that it's insensitive to cold, to warmth, or to touch…'

She was silent for a few seconds. There was no sound other than the hissing of the tea kettle through the open door of the nurse's room. Then she began again in a whisper:

'You see, the heart of the invalid sustains so many knife-wounds during a lifetime that it becomes scarred. Cicatrised… Insensitive to cold… to warmth… and to pain… Insensitive, dark, hardened…'

All this was said with a smile that betokened the most perfect inner calm.

From somewhere under the wardrobe Celina took out a gramophone and placed a record on it which Isa had chosen, a Bach organ concerto. Surely no music better complemented the sombre, stately red of the material on the walls or the grave but restful atmosphere of the room.

Before the music finished there was a knock on the door. It was a large woman in a green velvet dress, with fine-rimmed glasses that balanced precariously on the bridge of her nose and oscillated slightly with each step she took, like an instrument for registering an inner sensitivity barely detectable beneath the great slabs of fat layering her flesh.

'How are you, then? How are you feeling?' she panted breathlessly.

She enquired about Emanuel: who he was, where he came from, what illness he suffered from, which doctor took care of him. The questions poured out in an unending flood, as if they had previously been dammed up.

Isa explained everything with obvious boredom. The woman drank a cup of tea and wolfed down some dry cakes, one after the other, chewing up the words along with her food.

Emanuel was sorry that his visit had been interrupted so unpleasantly. Isa too flung up her hands several times in desperation. It was almost dinnertime. In the end the woman left, but not before having discharged a gust of good advice and encouragement.

'That woman is part of the team of professional comfort-givers in Berck. They are an extremely abject species of people who have absolutely nothing to do all day except come and bestow upon the patients a cheap dose of charity… They drink a cup of tea here, eat a sandwich there, then go home with their stomach full and their conscience satisfied that they have done a good deed…'

At that moment the attendant appeared to take them to the dining hall.

'I am sorry you could not stay longer,' she said. 'But you will come again, won't you?'

And at the moment the attendant began pushing the stretcher-bed.

'Do you want to be friends? Do you like it here in my room?'

'I like strange rooms that become familiar so quickly,' replied Emanuel, and felt his cheeks turning slightly red.

15

SPRING SLIPPED SLOWLY back into Berck. The rough vegetation of the dunes made a visible effort to become more delicate, and the sky itself shed its skin to reveal gentler colours. The beach expanded tumultuously, iridescent with the hues of an immense unburdening. The world weighed no more than vapour and light.

Emanuel went out regularly in his carriage, accompanied by Solange. Throughout the winter they had cultivated a calm, level-headed love in his room; now the trips to the countryside began anew.

His corset bothered him more and more, and apparently so did Solange. Emanuel would lift her dress entirely, uncovering her body, and kiss her dizzily on the chalk-white of her skin.

'Your body is my cleansing bath,' he would say, thinking of all the muck and mould he was wallowing in beneath his plaster.

There were cool and perfumed regions on her body around her hips, like the sudden breath of some new scent in the open air, coming from who knows where. They were pillows of comfort upon which he could rest his head. The blonde and warm tenderness of the rounded womb… the tiny shaded cup of the bellybutton, where Emanuel would pour a drop of clear water so that the belly became a landscape adorned with a fount in the middle of it.

All these games would become stupidly shipwrecked the next day when the attendant came in the morning to wash him; poking his fingers as far as they would go under the plaster, Emanuel would extract heaps of evil-smelling dirt and grime.

He locked the door during this abject and intimate activity so that no one would catch him in the act. Then, when he had done with this procedure, the attendant would turn him face down and insert a long, thin rod under the cast in order to scratch his back.

Tortured by the itching, Emanuel would wrench the rod from the attendant and frantically attempt to scratch himself until he was faint…

At the time in the afternoon when he knew Solange was due to arrive and he would be compelled to perform love's daily rituals, with the same caresses and the same kisses (because their love, like even the sweetest love in the world, had developed its own silly customs and ceremonies) he felt like running and hiding so that Solange would no longer find him.

Even his immense sense of admiration for her pure body began to annoy him. He was bored by her smooth skin and by their unclouded love, even by the simple gestures which she had learned from him in order to please him. In truth, he would have liked no longer to have to touch so much perfection. What good were the cleanliness and freedom of another body to him?

Everything that he did, he did quite as meticulously as on the first day of their love, because, as he liberated himself from each ritual, he could luxuriate in its absence and in how tiresome it had been… The more ceremoniously executed, he thought, the more exhilarating the freedom.

Over all these things, Solange's clear blue gaze roamed calmly and uncomprehendingly.

One day she received a worrying telegram from her grandfather, who was seriously ill. She was his only heir and the old man wanted to see her straight away. Solange left the same day. She and Emanuel agreed that she would call him on the third day, Saturday, at ten in the morning.

During his first day of solitude, Emanuel felt wonderful. He discovered that a free afternoon could be infinitely long and extremely pleasant… He divided up his time, he read, and went out in his carriage alone, free of the body that till then he had seemingly contained within his cast together with his own. At a tobacconist's he bought a lighter with a complicated mechanism, for which he had no need whatsoever, and afterwards sweets from a confectioner's. He secreted himself among the dunes, took the lighter from his pocket and, under the carriage's hood, he turned it on and off countless times, as if he had gone slightly mad, enjoying the flame, sharing this small amusement with himself, himself alone. He decided not to show it to

Solange when she returned and to keep it only for his own personal secret pleasure.

The next day, he took his carriage to the countryside by himself. The wind blew ferociously, nearly lifting the hood into the air; the horse ran aslant against the storm.

When he arrived at an inn he was drenched from the rain, he shivered from cold and his hands were frozen.

'Where is your fiancée?' asked the innkeeper.

'She's gone. I am by myself, as you can see,' replied Emanuel with obvious sadness.

He thought that the innkeeper could be his witness when he next came there with Solange: tell her, isn't it true that I was sad the day I came here without my fiancée?

And Solange would surely be flattered.

He asked for a dish of coffee and sipped it unhurriedly. He was all alone, with nothing to rush him: he didn't need to scald himself in order to finish his coffee faster so that they could get to the dunes, in fulfilment of their daily ritual. It was, undoubtedly, a very pleasant thing to make love, but Emanuel decided that it could be just as pleasant at times not to...

The day of the phone call came.

He went down to the office an hour before the appointed time, smoked the cigar which the director offered him out of politeness and which he accepted out of impertinence, read the newspapers, and was satisfied by how calmly he was waiting.

But the moment the phone rang, several minutes late, Emanuel felt himself suddenly seized by a terrible agitation.

'Hurry up! Hurry up!' he urged the attendant who was

positioning his trolley next to the telephone.

All the calm he had felt just a moment before had turned into sweeping impatience the instant the telephone rang, in the same way that a supersaturated solution suddenly crystallises on the introduction of a chemical substance.

He brought the receiver to his ear and realised that his hand was trembling, the receiver vibrating as if affected by a microscopic disturbance. Solange's voice burst through suddenly, very indistinct and metallic. But by what miraculous means was the room filled all at once with her presence? He was subject to a veritable invasion of sensations, filtering deep into his flesh, caused by nothing more than the buzzing of a distant and familiar voice…

'I need to stay another week, my grandfather has died, the funeral is tomorrow… I'm going insane with all the condolences, all the people, with sorting out the inheritance with the solicitor… I ran like a lunatic to get to the phone…'

She fell silent and Emanuel could hear in the receiver that she was out of breath. The same panting breath, but without her body. The essence of the pleasure he felt when he crushed her beneath his cast, but pure this time, without the body's obligation, without the effort…

'Why aren't you saying anything?' she asked, trying to still the trembling in her voice.

Emanuel shut his eyes and let himself be intoxicated by words.

'I want you to talk… tell me anything you want…' he murmured.

Solange began recounting a long argument she had with the notary… Emanuel found himself engulfed once more by his old desires, as if, along with her voice, the wire carried also the warmth of her skin, bringing it surging straight into his bloodstream…

He knew very well what he was doing, and, sliding his hand underneath the blankets as Solange continued to speak, he pounded his desperate arousal…

'Tell me something else, I implore you,' he insisted, a little light-headed, tormenting the flesh in comfortable, urgent pleasure.

She carried on speaking without suspecting anything.

Then, a moment later, her voice became ecstatic and Emanuel scattered himself in a brief, overwhelming moment of exhaustion, like a fainting fit.

'Thank you… thank you…' he murmured into the telephone.

'What for?' she asked, surprised.

'For everything you're telling me… for everything… for everything…'

Back in his room he ground his teeth in disgust at his indulging in such self-gratification.

He went, nevertheless, to the train station to wait for her, enacting to the end a simulacrum of perfect love. The moment she climbed into the carriage, he felt as if he had been stabbed through part of his plaster… Solange installed herself next to him on the seat and Emanuel smiled at her. On an empty side-street she leaned over him and kissed him on the mouth.

'All these days without you – it was as if I wasn't alive at all,' she murmured, looking into his eyes with the placid gaze of a devoted animal.

Emanuel shivered under the plaster with annoyance, with

disgust, and above all in reaction to the easy complaisance with which he accepted everything.

That same week an incident occurred at the beach that heightened his annoyance at her. There are certain situations that deteriorate of their own accord, through the daily incidents that accrue around them, in the same way that stones placed in calcareous waters become encrusted with lime simply by sitting in the stream. That day, as usual, Emanuel drove his horse far along the beach, well off the beaten track. The sea was approaching high tide and had flooded a good stretch of the sand. Solange advised him to turn around, but he was obstinate and insisted on pressing forward, believing he would find a path somewhere leading up the through the cliffs.

'I promise you there is no way up around here. I know the area very well,' Solange implored him. 'Before long we won't be able to turn around. The entire beach will be under water… Listen to me, Emanuel!'

It irritated him that she was right; he couldn't see a path going up through the cliffs anywhere. What vicious and sublime satisfaction for him, if only the way up could suddenly appear and in an instant they could be high above the coast!

Finally, tired and bored, he turned the carriage around. It was, however, a little too late. The ocean had invaded a large part of the beach and he was now compelled to guide the carriage carefully along a narrow strip of sand between channels of water.

In order to cut across more quickly he began to steer the carriage directly through the middle of the channels. Solange looked at him in horror. They suddenly found themselves facing a larger stretch of water, at which the horse stopped abruptly, refusing to advance.

'You'll never get through here,' said Solange. 'Don't you see how deep it is? Go round… Give me the reins!'

Emanuel, goaded to extreme fury, cracked his whip on the horse's back, and the carriage went forward into the water.

For several seconds the mare strained with all her might, but in the middle of the channel the carriage's wheels half sank into the waterlogged sand and would not go any further.

In desperation Emanuel jerked at the bridle and struck the horse, but to no avail. The situation was extremely serious: the carriage remained at a standstill, the sea was rising relentlessly, the waves were no more than ten metres away…

Pale with fright, Solange quickly shook off her shoes and stockings and ran, flying madly along the beach, looking for help. Emanuel lay inert in the carriage, stretched out face upward, his temples throbbing, overcome by excitement, irritation and fear.

The waves hissed in his ears like a storm that had got into his brains… as if all the blood in him, and the water, and the ocean and the air all began at once to boil and foam…

A minute later Solange returned with some sailors. The men opened the carriage and hauled Emanuel out along with the frame upon which he lay stretched, depositing him on the sand on the other side of the channel. Then they unharnessed the horse, and, heaving with all their might, pulled the carriage out of the water.

They all retreated toward the esplanade.

It was a procession that galled Emanuel to the core of his soul. The way he lay there on the frame, carried on the shoulders of the sturdy sailors, having narrowly escaped a horrible fate – it all followed the logical thread of his annoyance.

'That's all I needed… to owe her my gratitude!' he thought to himself, bitterly.

Solange led the column, barefoot, shoes and stockings in her hand. She was followed by the empty carriage, dragged slowly forward by two sailors with their trousers rolled up above their knees. Behind it came Emanuel, borne aloft on his frame, like a fallen hero upon his shield, and, finally, the horse, a young boy leading her by the bridle.

Behind them, children (where did they all come from?) and a few people, commenting on the adventure (where, where on earth had they suddenly appeared from?) 'Truly, the funeral of a great warrior,' thought Emanuel.

Solange turned her head in his direction from time to time, smiling with an innocence that burnt him to the quick.

Back at the sanatorium, he thanked her with effusive exaggeration so as to torment himself all the more cruelly.

And so as to inflict the maximum punishment on himself for his weakness during their telephone conversation, he reached in his pocket and took out his secret lighter, that was meant to be hidden from her sight:

'Do you like it?' he asked. 'I want you to have it…'

It is the last token that I will give to her, he thought to himself, the object that will bring an end to our idyll. Perhaps, if she hadn't accepted it, everything would have gone on as before… But the fact that she accepted it can only mean that our love must end, here and now…

The thought of their parting tormented him terribly. But Emanuel found it impossible to think of a solution. Leave the sanatorium? When? And where would he go? He must remain at Berck, and Solange would quickly find him.

Within the next few days, however, a completely unexpected solution intervened. Emanuel made his getaway from the sanatorium in so easy and surprising a fashion that for a long time he was amazed at the extraordinary nonchalance of his escape.

It was almost like a magic trick… Close your eyes, now open your eyes! One moment, he was in his room in the sanatorium, and the next, when he opened his eyes…

16

I N THE MONTH of May the tourist invasion began at Berck. The aspect of the whole town changed as if it had been overrun by barbarian hordes.

At the sanatorium, rooms were being prepared on the floors that had been unoccupied during winter.

An insufferable disturbance arose in the corridors and stairways: the floors were being scrubbed, pails filled with water lay strewn everywhere, doors slammed in a hurry, and the cleaning maids sweated profusely as they polished brassware on the elevator. Little by little the sanatorium was turning into a hotel. Patients were no longer allowed to park their trolleys in the corridors. That sort of thing could create the wrong impression with the summer guests.

Then erupted the gramophone. It began one evening with a clearly-heard humming, a tremulous melody on the cello, in a room lost somewhere on one of the floors, then on the next day the symphony swelled as a portable player reinforced the cello with a tune on the piccolos, and by the end of it, like a sudden stormy outburst in some Wagnerian opera, there came crashing from another room a ferociously thundering military fanfare... Room after room succumbed to the fearsome, all-consuming musical virus. Within a few days the entire sanatorium was vibrating frantically, a complex mishmash of orchestras, violins, marches and love songs. The building had become a colossal factory for wearing out gramophone records.

Maddened by lack of sleep, the patients plugged their ears with cotton or wax, or simply tied scarves around their heads.

Appalled, Emanuel took his carriage and left the hotel.

The beach too had been invaded. The cabins were lined up in an endless row, brought back to the beach from the waste ground where they had languished all winter among the weeds. Entire families lived inside the four wood plank walls, the doors left open to face the sea. People were doing their laundry there, and making jam; children whimpered while the father of the family, lying stretched out on the beach, read the newspaper and slowly slurped a cup of coffee mixed with sand. The beach itself was dug up, turned upside down, sculpted into ditches and trenches and castles... A gigantic clamour arose from its whole length, mixed with the desperate shouts of the vendors of beach-balls and sweets. From all corners, from all cabins, there was an unstoppable flood: streams of crumpled paper, rivers of old newspapers, paper, empty boxes, and yet more paper; an ocean of rubbish alongside the ocean's waves.

Emanuel looked for places to hide in the dunes, far from the car-filled main roads. There was a place beyond the town limits, quiet and wholly cut off from the traffic, where he would often go by himself. He had never taken Solange there. He had reserved this refuge for his own hours of absolute solitude. He would have liked to have remained there the whole time, hidden, never to return to the sanatorium. It was a wild spot, forsaken by humans. A few villas with peeling, ivy-covered walls rose out of the sand that half-buried them: but no one lived within. There had once been talk of building a train station there and creating a development of luxury villas, away from the rest of the town. The work had just begun when the war interrupted everything. It was still possible to see the rails running along the beach, the wheels of a few abandoned carriages among the weeds, and the tumbledown walls of the old station. On summer afternoons chickens pecked at the grass among the ruins while a cockerel climbed to the top of a wall and, beating his wings, let loose a discordant and prolonged cock-a-doodle-doo, like a desperate crying in the wilderness.

A solitary tavern, a tiny establishment with a verandah full of red geraniums, survived as a last sign of life… It was occasionally visited for a drink by sailors who had strayed in that direction with their fishing nets.

Emanuel made friends with the landlord. He spent long hours in front of the verandah on a sandy rise, from which he would stare far out into the ocean, lording over this place, with its villas ossified in the sand, its dilapidated station and the undulating expanse of dunes.

'A pity they never finished the station here… I'd have built the most beautiful hotel!' said the innkeeper, a tall man with a slight stoop, purple cheeks and white hair incessantly tousled by the wind. He wore in his eyes the melancholy calm of such abandoned places…

'Oh! If you only knew what a building site this used to be! What a bustle! What a hubbub! What an uproar! The prices for the lots went up to half a million…'

And then he added, sadly, 'Today you can't even get a thousand francs…'

The sailors would come with bags full of fresh sardines. The innkeeper's wife, a little, round ball of flesh and fat with a faded yellow wig on her head, haggled ferociously with them, partly out of miserliness and partly as a way to pass the time. She served Emanuel fresh fish, grilled on the coals.

Finally Emanuel came up with an idea. How nice it would be to live there at the tavern! Any room would do, no matter how tiny, no matter how uncomfortable, as long as it was isolated from the rest of the world. Several days had passed since the incident on the beach with Solange. He was certain she would never find him there in the dunes. He would disappear suddenly from the sanatorium and no one would know where he had gone. He asked the innkeeper. The man called his wife over to consult with her.

'It's not possible,' she answered. 'We live here by ourselves so as not to be bothered by anyone. We live a quiet life, you understand, and don't need either clients or lodgers.'

Emanuel was annoyed.

'Then is there no one living in those villas? No one at all?'

'Well, yes,' the innkeeper replied. 'Just in the one of them, that one over there…'

And he pointed to the roof of a stone villa sitting on a promontory above the coast, hidden behind some very high dunes.

'It's not occupied all year, though,' he added. 'An American woman comes with her son, just for the summer. They stay a few months and then they leave… They've been here a week now…'

Emanuel thought for a while.

'And this American lady… do you think it's possible she would let me stay there?' he asked. 'I'd pay her, of course, I'd pay her…'

The innkeeper and his wife gave an indulgent, ironic smile.

'She's a wealthy woman, Monsieur! Why would she need to take in lodgers, especially sick ones? And when all's said and done, why do you want to live here in these abandoned parts anyway?' the tavern keeper asked inquisitively.

'Well, that's another matter!' replied Emanuel. 'But how could I talk to her? Should I go there in my carriage?'

The innkeeper was taken aback:

'In your carriage, do you say? But can't you see there are dunes as high as the house all the way there? Can you climb up the dunes? Is your horse an acrobat?'

'You say she's been there a week?' asked Emanuel, deep in thought. 'Do you think she's at home now?'

'Maybe, I don't know,' replied the innkeeper.

'Well then, I'll go and see her and talk to her,' said Emanuel calmly, taking the reins in his hands.

'What?' said the innkeeper. 'In your carriage?' and he looked at Emanuel in amazement.

'Certainly, in my carriage… Well, I'm not going there on foot!'

'I'd like to see you try!' challenged the innkeeper, beginning to laugh.

'All right, let's see!' replied Emanuel, accepting the challenge.

He tightened his grip on the reins and took off toward where the first dune rose up. Only a few days had passed since his accident on the beach, but the memory hardly affected him at all.

He began to urge on his horse. The slope was gradual enough and the horse made it easily to the ridge.

When he reached the top, Emanuel turned his head toward the tavern keeper and waved to him.

'Farewell! Farewell! I am off to the high mountains!'

The innkeeper, his wife and a couple of sailors that had come out of the tavern, stood together on the verandah, gazing open-mouthed at the extraordinary dune-clambering carriage.

Before him stretched a flat strip of sand, followed by much taller slopes; an entire row, as if purposefully placed there as a barrier.

Emanuel had embarked on an adventure which he was by no means going to renounce. Ambition spurred him on, and so, especially, did a terrific curiosity to see the owner of the villa.

The tavern had disappeared behind the sands; there was nothing left to do but go boldly forward…

He stopped a short distance before the slopes. He waited a few minutes to give the mare a rest, then tugged abruptly at the reins. The horse again reached the top in one go.

The rest was child's play; they crossed the last few ups and downs to get to the villa with ease.

He found himself facing the building; the shutters were closed, the gate locked. Could the innkeeper have played a joke on him? Was the villa empty? He began knocking on the gate with his whip handle; the knocks reverberated all around, their echoes like shouted orders repeated from dune to dune. There was a burst of barking in the courtyard and immediately one of the shutters opened.

A red-haired woman in a violet dressing-gown appeared in the window frame:

'What is it? Who's there?' she shouted as she looked around the courtyard to see who had knocked.

All of a sudden she spotted Emanuel in his carriage in front of the gate. She was astonished.

'What is it?' she asked in amazement. 'What do you want? And how did you manage to get here in your carriage?'

Emanuel wanted to shout but the baying of the dog was louder than his voice; he waved to the woman to come down.

A boy of about fifteen, tall and sturdy, his hair the same colour of red as the woman's, unlocked the gate. Emanuel drove his carriage into the little cemented courtyard as the dog leapt about him with a deafening bark.

'Hush... Hush!' the boy quietened the animal, grabbing it by the scruff of the neck and wrestling with it. It was an enormous black dog, almost as tall as its master when it stood on its hind legs with its paws on his shoulders.

Emanuel studied the villa. The building appeared to be neglected rather than old. A nameplate was fixed to the roof just below its peak, rusty and covered with ivy. He made out the name: Villa Elseneur.

At last, the lady at the window also made her appearance. She had tidied her hair a little and had probably powdered herself. Emanuel caught on the wind a vague breath of feminine scent, sweetish and pleasant.

'What do you want?' she asked.

Emanuel introduced himself. She extended her hand, told him her name, Mrs Tils, and abruptly asked in a highly familiar tone:

'How do you do?'

It was the English-speaking custom to use this formula, even when addressing a stranger.

'Forgive me for disturbing you so early in the morning,' said Emanuel. 'I was just passing by in my carriage.'

'In your carriage…?' she repeated, incredulous.

'And I love this area, I can't tell you how much. I was told that this is the only inhabited villa and… I should like to ask you something…'

Emanuel hesitated, then spoke what he had to say rapidly, in order to get over having to utter it, the same way one drinks down bitter medicine in one gulp.

'Look here… if it is at all possible… I'd like to live here… I love this solitude. You wouldn't allow me to live in your villa… you wouldn't be willing to accept a lodger?'

'Is that why you wanted to talk to me?' said the lady, bursting merrily into laughter.

Emanuel looked so utterly bewildered that he could do nothing but cause amusement. He noticed that her cheeks revealed deep wrinkles when she laughed. She was certainly an elderly woman, but she possessed an admirable naturalness of gesture and a well-maintained youthful appearance.

'I am so sorry,' she said, 'but I can't take on lodgers. I never have, and wouldn't know how to go about such things.'

While she was talking, a tremendous racket suddenly burst from the upstairs window, which had been left open: shouting and screaming, like the cursing of a cantankerous old woman bickering sharply with someone.

Emanuel looked at the window in puzzlement, but without asking any question. She noticed his surprise: 'You know… I don't live here alone. Apart from my son Irving and the cook, I have a guest… As you can see, he's a very irritable personage, he shouts and swears something terrible…'

'Irving, why don't you go and get him?'

The boy went into the house. The shouting ended, and after a few seconds, Irving came down with a parrot in his hand.

'Say "good morning",' commanded Mrs Tils.

The parrot let loose a formidable curse. Everyone burst out laughing. The parrot pecked at Mrs. Tils' hair, pulling at it with all its might. A dog, a parrot… Emanuel was upset that he couldn't live there. He decided to leave.

'And how will you get back?'

'The way I came, straight over the dunes…'

Irving wanted to help Emanuel in his ascent of the dunes.

'Bravo! Bravo!' he shouted, clapping his hands, when Emanuel reached the top of a ridge.

That afternoon, as he was wandering morosely through the streets, and had stopped his carriage at a shop window, someone came up to speak to him. It was Mrs Tils, though Emanuel almost didn't recognise her in her outdoor clothes.

'I wanted to tell you something… You see, I've changed my mind, and I would be willing to let you stay at the villa… if in exchange you could give maths lessons to my son… I have a large room, a hall looking out to the sea. Are you any good at maths?'

Emanuel assured her that he had given maths lessons before, and happily accepted. He had a strong sense that, since the morning, the course of the day's events had assumed a delightful fragility, full of surprises.

He let himself be led by circumstance, feeling a delicate pleasure within himself: 'So when can I come with my luggage, Madame?'

'Whenever you wish,' she replied. 'Tomorrow, even…'

'Then please expect me at ten in the morning…'

17

AND WHEN HE opened his eyes…

The room in which he found himself was enormous, with doors opening toward the ocean. Pictures in the English style hung on the walls in frames of faded gold. One depicted an imposing hunting scene with riders in red coats gathered in a clearing in the woods and surrounded by packs of dogs and beaters blowing their brass horns, while another portrayed an elderly, white-haired man in a nightshirt getting ready for bed, the fine skin of his cheeks exceedingly wrinkled, as always with old men in engravings. In the background you could see his old-fashioned bed with its bedposts and floral cretonne curtains.

The ocean waves thundered riotously in the vast room. The day hung heavily from ashen clouds suspended like a roof over the dunes.

Emanuel studied the pictures on the walls. Here was his own situation, synthesised in these two engraved scenes. The little old man getting ready for sleep was himself, in the present solitude of the Villa Elseneur. Just like the old man, withdrawn from the world, in a strange room, peaceful and alone amidst outmoded furniture. And next to it, the hunting scene, whose hubbub the old man seemed to avoid by turning his back on it, was a perfect representation of the uproar in the town which Emanuel had fled.

The heavy curtains of cherry velvet blew in the wind like the funeral banners that hang in mortuaries. Emanuel shut his tired eyes. Everything had happened like a miracle, and between morning, when he had packed his bags in his hotel bedroom, and now, late in the afternoon, when he found himself amidst the dunes, a lodger of Mrs Tils, the day had changed its countenance entirely, as if it was now part of another year, another season, another reality... Who would have suspected that he, Emanuel, who had always been Emanuel, would be hiding here, lost amidst the waves of sand? It was as if he had exchanged his identity...

He lay in a corner of the hall, a little bewildered, like a creature hurled by the ocean into a cleft in the rocks. He too was waiting motionless for a wave that would rescue him and tow him out, back to the fullness of life, back to a world he could fully make sense of.

He recalled the events that had taken place during the last two days as if they were ancient history: how he had notified the director of his departure the very moment he returned from the town after his conversation with Mrs Tils; how he had packed his bags in a hurry.

'And what is your new address?' the director had asked.

'There's no point in giving it to you,' replied Emanuel. 'I'll come in person now and then to pick up any correspondence.'

And then how he had arrived at Villa Elseneur at precisely ten in the morning as promised. Irving, the cook and the innkeeper, who had come to lend a hand, helped him up the steps. The innkeeper in particular was extremely surprised that Mrs Tils had taken him in as a lodger.

'Did you really not know her before?' he kept whispering, trying to pry an answer from Emanuel.

'No! Really!' Emanuel replied in irritation. 'Don't I know what's true here and what isn't?'

Now he was waiting for supper. Darkness had fallen completely. It was high tide, and the sea came up to the feet of the cliffs, dashing against the sea wall with a muffled, rhythmic thundering. He had spent the entire day by himself in the immense, empty room. From time to time he could hear the parrot's raucous, syllabic crowing coming from upstairs, and from outside the occasional dog bark.

Where was the sanatorium now? And Solange? In the room's airy silence no image of them was strong enough to coalesce into a solid consistency.

The cook brought a lamp and put it, lit, on the table. Around the lampshade a wheel of light spread out on the plush carpet, a minuscule circus ring in which coloured velvet flowers executed strange, motionless acrobatic feats…

The days were warm and Emanuel rested on the terrace fronting the room. The expanse of sea glittered like a fantastic ball gown, spangled with diamonds, foaming with lace. The brightness of the water became a viscous radiance that blinded the eyes. Immense spots of light melted away in the air, leaving behind them incorporeal, green contours, and in the distance the waves darkened to a cobalt blue…

He and Mrs Tils often talked together. She told him about her husband, whom she had accompanied to Berck, a sufferer like Emanuel from Pott's disease, who had died eight years before, there at Villa Elseneur. He too had enjoyed the solitude of the dunes; he too had driven his carriage over them one day and stopped, enchanted, in front of the villa, no longer wishing to live anywhere else but there. He had bought it from the commune for next to nothing. He too had had his room in the hall facing out to sea.

'I'll tell you why I took you on as a lodger,' she said. 'When I saw how sad you were that you couldn't live here, I remembered my husband's melancholy and his terrible thirst for solitude. It was in his memory that I took you in… In his memory, and, because, in this villa in which he died… I would like a young man to get well…'

She spoke with simplicity and in a tone of great devotion. The friendship she bestowed on Emanuel was spontaneous and naïve, similar to the love she bore for her dog, her son or her parrot, and she used the same expressions and the same tone of voice to all of them.

The days passed in sunlight and quiet. Solange… where could

Solange be? It had been almost a month since he had moved to the villa, and he had had no news of her.

In the old building's outdated atmosphere, in the transparency of the life he now led, not a shadow ever returned to haunt him of that which had silently passed over him before.

He lay in the sun, diffuse, covered in light, clear and transparent like water in which no image can leave its trace.

He realised now how profound and fragile their love had been.

And how fragile had been his very life till then; how insubstantial was the entire reality of the days that had passed by him like a quietly-flowing river, whose current he could feel within himself when he lay motionless and eyes shut. One day he wrote to Dr Cériez, inquiring when and where he might come for an examination. He received a short answer:

Vanished friend,

Come whenever you want to the sanatorium clinic, but tomorrow at ten in the morning is best. I wonder how you discovered Villa Elseneur. Give my regards to Mrs Tils.

Dr Cériez

Emanuel was surprised. How did the doctor come to know Mrs Tils? He asked her this.

'He was one my husband's best friends. He came to see us often,' she replied. 'He knew these parts well and would surely have lived around here if he hadn't been a doctor. He too suffers from the enchantment of the wilderness…'

The next day Emanuel sent Irving to town to fetch a carriage. It was brought to the tavern door, and Emanuel was carried there over the dunes on a stretcher. That morning the clinic was deserted. He proceeded to the examination room the moment he arrived. The consultation lasted no more than a few minutes. Dr Cériez examined the abscess attentively, inserted his hand under the plaster and felt the vertebrae.

'I think that we can remove your corset,' he said. 'And in a month or two you will begin, perhaps, to walk again.'

'You can remove my cast?' Emanuel asked, giddy with happiness. 'Is it true?'

In the months that he had worn the cast on his body, he had become so accustomed to it that he did not even imagine that one day it might be removed. Besides, he had come to see this misery as an organic function, intolerable but permanent. To feel freedom once more in his body seemed a thing extraordinary, a fresh start in life, a new birth into the world.

'Is it really true, then?' he murmured in a daze.

'Yes… We'll remove it on Saturday morning.'

And the doctor shook his hand and left the room, superb, tall, magnificent with his leonine mane, like a bountiful giant scattering miracles about him.

Emanuel waited a few minutes in the corridor for the attendant to come and take him to his carriage.

'Caught you!' exclaimed somebody behind him, covering his eyes with his hands.

For a moment Emanuel was frightened. He thought it was Solange, but the hands smelt strongly of tobacco. It was Ernest.

'Where've you escaped to? When and how did you leave? You know, your disappearance caused a huge sensation at the sanatorium!'

Ernest touched his chest, his hands, as if he couldn't believe that he had found him again.

'I can tell you, I looked for you at all the sanatoria in town... I searched clinic after clinic... boarding house after boarding house... I even went to the police... Where have you been? Where were you hiding?'

Emanuel affected a slightly enigmatic air. It was an awfully pleasant morning, the doctor had told him the cast was coming off, Ernest was intrigued with his disappearance ...

'And do you know who made me do all that searching?' he continued. 'Do you know who the eagerest person to find you was in the whole sanatorium?'

'Who?'

'Guess!'

Emanuel paused for thought.

'I'll tell you... Isa!' exclaimed Ernest. 'She was burning with curiosity!'

Emanuel felt that the morning was becoming ever more agreeable.

Just then, Celina happened to walk past in the corridor.

'What's this I see?' she exclaimed, frozen to the spot, hands on her chest like a beetle with its elytra folded. 'Not Monsieur Emanuel? Where have you popped up from? I'm going straight off to tell Mademoiselle Isa the news! But I will let her know... little by little, so she won't be taken by surprise, all at once. She has been suffering for some time now... she has a permanent fever...'

'May I see her?' asked Emanuel.

'Let me go and ask her. She hadn't woken up when I left to go to town…'

Celina returned a few minutes later.

'She's expecting you and Monsieur Ernest.'

Isa did indeed look very tired; a gentle somnolence veiled her eyes. 'Where have you been hiding? Where did you run off to?' she asked Emanuel.

The room smelled vaguely of disinfectant and festering matter. It was the sharp odour of rotting vegetables that erupted in the summer from the rooms of patients with abscesses; the scent that Celina had sprayed a few minutes before was unable to hide it completely.

Isa was holding an album in her hands.

'I was looking at some old photographs… Look, this is me…'

She handed the album, open, to Emanuel. A nearly faded photograph showed a little girl of about two in a park with statues and snow-covered trees. Her face was so small and eyes so wide with astonishment that she looked like a doll.

'I wonder what I was thinking about when they took the picture,' said Isa. 'What cause for astonishment had the world presented me with at that instant?'

She went on, more sadly:

'Ah! that pure and naïve moment caught in the photograph! What horrible deceit! How much anguish followed…'

Ernest, too, stared long at the photograph.

Celina opened the window; the garden was filled with patients and holidaymakers. Emanuel cast an uneasy glance at all these noisy crowds.

How sheltered from them he felt now! A gramophone began metallically, scratchily, to contribute its own piece of the noise. But that wasn't all… ten or so portable gramophones were set up on a number of tables. A few young men and women were changing the records on each one; they had invented something new.

'They came up with a stupid game a few days ago,' said Isa. 'They set up their gramophones in a row and begin playing all of them at the same time… ten gramophones… ten different records…'

And indeed, all at once, a formidable cacophony of sounds and howls blasted out of the ten machines as they began to play simultaneously…

'And what does the director say? And the patients?' Emanuel was shouting in order to be heard.

'The patients plug their ears with cotton,' Isa explained. 'As for the director, he says nothing so as not to lose customers.'

There was a chaotic outpouring of notes, a jumble of pieces of music, like the explosion of a thunderstorm that the whole atmosphere has long been hatching and which is now let loose all at once with howls, yells and deafening bangs.

'Shut the window! Shut it!' Isa cried out in horror.

'Why don't you move to another sanatorium?' asked Emanuel.

'It's the same everywhere,' said Ernest. 'It's a well-known fact that in summer the town belongs to the living…'

Celina brought coffee for everyone.

They talked about the patients in the sanatorium.

'And Tonio?' asked Emanuel, who had not seen him for a long time.

Ernest had the most recent information about him.

'I can tell you the latest news... One of his brothers came here to pick up a suitcase with some books Tonio had left behind at the sanatorium... He told me sensational things about him, absolutely sensational...'

'What exactly? Quick, tell us,' Isa insisted impatiently.

'You know that after Madame Wandeska's departure he left as well, went to Paris, to stay with his brother... He'd begun drinking while still at Berck... but in Paris he crawled from one bar to the next. His brother tried to put some sense into him, in vain; all the advice, all the threats were in vain...

One evening something extraordinary happened to him... His brother laughed while he told me about his adventure, but myself I found it frightening... Poor Tonio!'

He fell silent for a few seconds. 'So, one evening after drinking his fill (and maybe a good deal more), he walked the streets like a madman for a while, then went to sleep on a bench by a metro station.

'Suddenly he had a fit of liver pain – it's a common thing with alcoholics – and he began howling from the pain, shrieking, and, drunk as he was, rolling around on the floor. It was two in the morning. A policeman came past on his beat and, seeing a man writhing on the asphalt, tried to interrogate him, but couldn't understand one word of what he was muttering.

'Of course, he was clearly drunk, but his howls of pain sounded more like the cries of a wounded man... The policeman called two passers-by to help him and Tonio was carried off to a nearby clinic.

'They quickly found an available room for him and the night porter went to find the doctor on duty.

'All this time the fit had subsided a little, the pain had probably gone away, in any case, no one can tell exactly what happened, but when Tonio opened his eyes in the strange room, he was seized by a blind fury.

'He got up from his bed, began to throw everything, mattresses, pillows, onto the floor, to bash the chairs against the walls, then, finding a pair of bandage scissors left, who knows why, in the drawer of a table, he grabbed them and went out in the hall, ready to plunge them into the first man who got in his way. He was foaming with fury; the alcohol was boiling in him fiendishly... he found a half-open door, where a faint sliver of light leaked out into the corridor... And then, something unexpected happened, something terrifying and ridiculous, to round off the adventure with an utterly grotesque finale: Tonio pushed the door open and found the room completely empty. He spotted a photograph of a woman on the wall, grabbed it and cut it to bits with the scissors. The room belonged to a nurse who was taking care of a gravely ill patient... The door to the neighbouring room was open and you could hear the dying man's wheezing. The nurse had left for a few moments and was about to come back. Tonio, his scissors raised threateningly... looking a fright... went into the dying patient's room and suddenly found himself face to face with a weak old man raised up on his pillows, with a hideous face and one of his eyes leaking... He was sitting up in bed, fingering his prayer beads and murmuring litanies, his voice cracking and wheezing... His good eye had kept all its vigour and sharpness. It was a bulbous, cold stare that pinned Tonio in the doorway.

'I want to kill a man ...' he mumbled vaguely and dropped the scissors.

The old man was puzzled, he calmly put the beads down and very quietly beckoned with his hand:

'Come closer, young man... very... amusing... very amusing ...'

'The poor patient was terribly bored during his long nights of insomnia and now, when finally something interesting was going on in his room, he wanted to see this phenomenon more closely.

'Come here, young man... don't be... afraid...'

'Tonio, shattered by the paroxysm of the fit that had now passed, fell wearily onto a chair near the bed. The patient's nurse, who had come in behind him a moment before and witnessed the last few seconds of the episode, went looking for help in order to get Tonio out of the room.

'When she came back, she found a scene that might have been very moving, if it hadn't been so grotesque at the same time... the little one-eyed old man, sitting up in his bed, counting his beads and reciting the Ave Maria in a loud voice, with Tonio, the former vicious assassin, sitting next to him as good as gold, and calmly, in the quiet voice of an obedient student, repeating the prayers under the hypnotic, fixed gaze of the single, unwavering eye... That's what his brother told me...'

Ernest ended his tale.

They were all silent, moved by the story. Emanuel looked at his watch. It was time for him to go.

'I will probably be here on Saturday,' he told Isa. 'I'm coming to the clinic to "shed" my cast,' he added with glee.

He was in a particularly good mood. The attendant came and Emanuel let himself be wheeled away, completely pleased with the morning, exulted by the thought that soon he would be free of the corset.

He was thinking of that and so many other agreeable things when suddenly, as he got to the back of the courtyard where his carriage was, his eyes flew wide open in bewilderment... It was too late to run away...

On a stool in the carriage, quite calmly holding a newspaper in her hands, Solange was waiting...

18

EMANUEL, FOR HIS part, tried to keep calm too.

'I saw you going into the clinic,' she said. Forgive me for waiting for you. If I'm bothering you, I'll go...'

It was true that he had found her sitting quietly on the stool when he arrived, absorbed in reading the newspaper, but her quivering voice and the rapid breathing that was intensifying beneath her blouse (you could almost see her heart beating) betrayed all her suppressed emotion.

Emanuel didn't have the courage to be impolite in broad daylight, face to face. While the attendant loaded him into the carriage, he asked her to come along with him: 'I have to talk to you, to explain,' he said.

As soon as they were alone, he discovered to his surprise that he had nothing to say to her. What exactly should he explain to her?

There was, somewhere in the dunes, a villa called Elseneur. He liked it there. He was alone. He spent entire hours sitting out in the sun on the terrace; he had found peace and quiet again… What did all these things have to do with Solange? He agonised over trying to find words clear or appropriate enough. He racked his brains to no avail; nothing came to him, absolutely nothing…

He told himself he would say nothing till he had finished counting to a hundred. Solange sat next to him, equally silent, with a slightly distracted gaze and her mouth clenched, the way she froze in silence when she was troubled by a thought.

Slowly, step by step, the horse pulled the carriage along the streets of a town as silent as he. The animal's hooves beat upon the silence, shattering it loudly and clearly and as if exasperating it. Their whole inability to speak found its rhythm in the steady tempo of these blows on the cobblestones.

'What could I tell her?' worried Emanuel to himself, and he suddenly felt a solidarity with the houses around him, with their drawn awnings, with the impassiveness of the trees and the utter perplexity of all these places that had no need to explain themselves to anyone.

'There will eventually come a moment, later on, when Solange will no longer be next to me. I will stretch out my hand, for instance, and the stool will be empty and I will be alone again… It's a matter of putting up with the silence for a while,' Emanuel told himself, and the thumping at his temples increased more and more from all the frustration and the throbbing tension of his clenched jaw.

'So where are you staying?' Solange finally asked.

Ah! Did someone speak? Emanuel was startled. In the carriage, in the drive through back streets, in the rhythm of the hooves on the asphalt, it seemed that the possibility of uttering a word had dissolved away for ever.

He burst into a long description of the Villa Elseneur. He told her how well he felt there; he described Mrs Tils, the cook, the innkeeper... He told her the story of how he got there... His previous reserve had required but a single word in order to evaporate into this light chatter. The dense block of silence needed no more than a slight fissure to cause everything inside to come flooding out.

It was, in the end, the same impatience with the irritation of having to speak, existing in the same way as the constraint that had caused him to say nothing. Solange grabbed hold of the reins to stop the horse. They had left the town too far behind on their way to the dunes and she wanted to go back. A beggar crossed the road. Solange stopped him to give him some money. Emanuel now had an opportunity to observe just how changed she was. She searched the purse with her hands, staring into emptiness like a blind woman rummaging through her things, while the light in her eyes remained lifeless, diluted to nothing.

Emanuel took out his wallet as well. The moment he opened it a tiny piece of carefully folded paper fell out. Solange resurfaced from the depths of her preoccupation and fixed her gaze on the piece of paper.

'A love note?' she asked.

Emanuel finally realised what virulent poison had been filtering through her silence till then. Had Solange really uttered those words? In an instant a sign of her inner despair manifested itself, and on her pallid cheeks, like the stigmata of misery, two spots of violent red appeared.

'Solange, what's wrong…?'

She was silent for a few seconds, then took a deep breath and spoke slowly, like the distant echo of an unseen tumult.

'My soul has frozen, Emanuel… Something has frozen in me… I feel cold… something inside me is cold.' And she pointed to her chest with her hand. 'What is that note?'

Emanuel hesitated.

'Forgive me, but I can't tell you.' Then, with a quick movement, he put it back in his wallet. He regretted terribly that he couldn't show it to her. It was the piece of bone given to him by Quitonce. He hadn't touched the tiny packet since the day after the operation when Quitonce had given it to him; he had a profound horror of opening it up.

'It's impossible for me to show it to you, but I can tell you what it contains…'

Solange stepped down from the carriage:

'Thank you… I don't need to know any more…'

She put out her hand, a hand soft and slightly damp, that Emanuel held in his for a few seconds like a little animal, dead but still warm.

'Farewell, Emanuel…'

'Why farewell?' he asked, surprised.

Suddenly uneasy, he added:

'I'd like us to see each other again… to remain friends…'

She looked at him as if she didn't know that he was there.

'Farewell. I'm saying farewell.'

And she left, turning away sharply at the exact instant that tears welled up in her eyes.

The next day was the anniversary of the late Mr Tils' death. Preparations for the pilgrimage from Villa Elseneur to the cemetery began early in the morning. Emanuel hadn't slept well. He had had terrible nightmares, and the memory of his dreams persisted like a shadow in the morning light.

The entire villa was fragrant with the heavy scent of lilies and narcissi that had been brought in the day before. It was a day of precise rituals, in which everyone ate only frugally; Mrs Tils lay weeping on the bed in her room upstairs, drenching one handkerchief after another in tears; the cook performed all her duties, dusting, serving the tea, dressed in black and with a ridiculous toque on top of her coiffed head, while Irving fitted the dog with a muzzle to prevent it from barking. The air smelled sweet and funereal from the mass of flowers that had been gathered up into bouquets. At ten in the morning everyone made ready to leave. A difficulty presented itself: the cemetery was far and they wouldn't return until late in the afternoon. Who would take care of Emanuel? The cook would not forego the ceremony for anything. It was no use Emanuel asking her to postpone her pilgrimage till the following day, since surely her bouquet would do just as much good on the grave then.

'Monsieur's anniversary is today and you want me to go there tomorrow? What good would that be? What good are my flowers on any other day of the year?'

It was as if the invisible spirit of the deceased had arranged for everyone to gather at his grave on the precise anniversary of his death. On any other day flowers would be useless because his spirit would not be there.

'Monsieur cared so much for me,' the woman said, bursting into tears.

'Well then, I'll stay here by myself,' said Emanuel. 'In fact, I won't need anything, and I don't suppose the house will catch fire today of all days...'

They left a little bag of food for his lunch on a table next to him and placed him in his carriage at the far end of the room so he would not be burnt by the sun. They drew the curtains and Emanuel was left in the coolness of the room, in the villa's absolute solitude...

This was the first time that he had found himself completely alone in the building. When he saw everyone disappearing beyond the dunes, he was seized by a vague sense of disquiet.

The door opening onto the terrace had been left ajar and a weak breath of hot air blew in from the noonday swelter outside, causing the curtains to stir slightly. It would have been better, perhaps, for the door to be closed. Any other day, when he could have called for someone, he would doubtless not have noticed the movement. Now, on the other hand, simply because he couldn't move from his stretcher-bed in order to close the door, the useless and repetitive agitation of the billows of velvet on the other side of the room aggravated him dreadfully.

With his arms hanging down, he attempted to reach the wheels of the stretcher-bed so as to direct it towards the door, but he only succeeded in getting himself much more irritated and working himself into a hot sweat. The day had congealed in the oppressive, suffocating heat. The sea's slothful splashing could be heard beneath the terrace, like gasps of laboured breath. Everything that happened was muffled and subdued. Beneath his plaster, Emanuel lay smouldering in acidic, clammy perspiration.

Suddenly, on one of the dunes on the way from the tavern, the postman appeared. 'Ah, excellent!' thought Emanuel, 'I can ask him to close the door…'

The postman usually went round the villa and gave Mrs Tils' mail to the cook. Emanuel had never yet received any post, but this time the postman headed directly for the terrace.

'I have a letter for you,' he said as he came in, red-faced and drenched in sweat.

'For me?' Emanuel asked in surprise.

It was a large envelope, with a black border and a typewritten address. The postman hurried off towards the tavern, looking forward to a break.

'Please do shut the door,' Emanuel cried out after him.

When he was alone at last, he tore the envelope open. The shock left him aghast. He would have liked to have yelled out to call the postman back, but it was too late. The dunes lay deserted in the sun, and no matter how loudly he shouted, no one would have heard him. He had stupidly shut himself in the room, as if in a trap. He should have had the presence of mind to open the envelope while the postman was still there… Now it was too late. He turned the letter, with its bitter, laconic content, over and over in his hand. The edges were decorated with a few macabre drawings, a skull and crossbones, a skeleton, and in the centre was a single line:

When you read these words… Farewell! Solange

Emanuel lay back exhausted, feeling drained of all his strength. The heat outside became terribly dry. There was not a drop of saliva left in his mouth. The emotion choked him like a lump in his throat.

He would have preferred the meaning of the letter he was turning over and over in his hands to have been less clear. He was especially annoyed by the pictures, badly drawn and no doubt sketched in a hurry. Oh! so that's why Solange had left with such a sad air the day before. Now he understood everything.

Where was she that very moment? Was she lying on her deathbed in her room in the boarding house, or wheezing in a convulsion of choking, eyes rolling in her head, surrounded by the throngs of concierges and curious passers-by that invariably accompany any such headline news?

Perhaps there was still time to save her. In these cases a single moment could be of crucial importance. He thought of crawling, on his belly, over the dunes, to the tavern, in order to send someone to the town, but the plaster corset clasped him to his trolley like a claw gripping him tightly, leaving no hope of escape. Again and again, to give himself some feeble reassurance, he told himself that the note was not so ominous and sinister, but whenever he took it from the table and examined it anew, he found in it yet more desperation and madness than before.

In vain he tried to close his eyes and wait… no one can measure the passage of time with his own pulse. Around him things lay in a state of suspension and stifling heat. All his struggling efforts melted languidly away in the massive, feeble listlessness of that day. He had a powerful feeling that the intense concentration with which he focused on the faintest sound coming from the dunes was vanishing uselessly into thin air, evaporating in the heat. It was a strange sensation, as when in a dream the unleashing of a powerful force ends only in weak dissipation. The landscape had become deserted to the point of desolation, while his impatience withered away all the more within him, the single focus of this infuriating day.

He lay there hallucinating, staring with eyes wide open through the glass door at the thin line of the blue horizon that delimited the sand, until the shapes of the dunes shattered like glass into shards of light that stabbed him in the eye.

Nothing will happen if you wait for it too impatiently, he told himself. The intensity of the waiting pushes away all objects that fall into its spin like a waterspout... Until I've calmed down myself, they won't come back...

And he tried without success to stop fretting.

Within the confines of this day, he mused, lie both my impatience and whatever happens with Solange. What is she doing now? Is she dead? Is she alive?

Perhaps weeping would have helped, but that would have been too focused an action amidst the enervating tranquillity of everything around him...

When, an hour later, they all returned from the cemetery, Emanuel had only strength left weakly to ask Irving to make haste to the town on his bicycle: 'If her room is locked, have it forced open,' said Emanuel in a feeble voice. 'Have them look for her… look for her everywhere, it's extremely serious. And if you find Madame Solange, give her this letter…'

He scrawled a few words in hurry that even he could not really understand…

19

EVERY EVENING, BEFORE going to bed, Mrs Tils came to Emanuel's room to chat a little and wish him good night.

But that evening, fatigued after the pilgrimage to the cemetery, she excused herself from her visit to his room. Emanuel, too, was worn out from the day's emotional excitement. Irving had returned with the message that the lady to whom the note had been addressed had left her lodgings around midday and had not yet returned... It was still light outside when everyone at Villa Elseneur went to bed after a day full of exhausting adventures.

Emanuel had requested that the heavy velvet curtains be drawn, so as to make his room as dark as possible, but light from the terrace penetrated through, and for a long time he lay tormented by insomnia. The clear blue of the summer evening buzzed outside his closed eyelids.

He finally fell into a deep, dreamless slumber. An hour later he woke up drenched in a puddle of sweat. He turned on the light and looked at his watch. It was ten o'clock. It was dark outside and a profound stillness reigned over the villa.

He tried to read, but without success: there was too much silence, and the words were so smooth and round that they detached themselves from the page and turned into nonsense.

All of a sudden he heard steps on the cement in the courtyard. Irving had locked up the dog to prevent it barking. He could clearly hear someone walking around, trying the window, then the door.

He was on the point of calling out for someone when the doorbell rang stridently.

'Who is it?' shouted Emanuel.

No answer came from outside. The bell continued to ring, more insistently. Now the cook had woken up and was coming down the corridor, shuffling in her slippers.

'Is this Villa Elseneur?' came a voice from the outside, in which Emanuel recognised nothing familiar.

The cook opened the door a crack and exchanged a few whispers with the person who had rung, then came to Emanuel's room and knocked quietly.

'What is it?' he asked in surprise.

'Someone has come to see you… Says they need to speak to you immediately.' The cook came into the room. 'It's a young lady… who… a girl… but she appears to me to be a bit…' and she made a gesture pointing to her forehead… 'says that you asked for her.'

Only now did Emanuel remember Solange.

'Very well, tell her to come in…'

He pushed the lamp toward the middle of the table and turned up the flame; all at once the room lit up, like a man raising his eyebrows in anticipation of a surprise.

In the doorway stood Solange.

It was indeed she, but the servant had been right to doubt her sanity. Her whole face was sullied with mud and water, her dress hung in tatters and her hair was undone and strewn with sand. What filth had she wallowed in, to end up looking like a mad street beggar? Emanuel's heart constricted with a pang yet more agonising than when the letter had arrived.

And that was not all.

Only after she entered the room did he glimpse in her hands the hideous objects she had brought with her, scavenged, no doubt, from some waste-ground. In one hand she clutched an old torn and rotting shoe, and in the other, a dead bird, its neck hanging down, featherless and horrific.

Emanuel was aghast. Solange, her mouth half open (a thread of saliva trickled from the corner of her lips), stood there frozen, her gaze weak, dreadfully clouded and vacant. 'What is it? What has happened?' Emanuel wanted to shout out loud in order to wake her up, to grab her by the hand and shake her briskly back to reality.

'I brought you these...' she said, and placed the dead bird and the shoe on the table.

The colour had completely drained from her face, which bore an ashen, ill-defined pallor, like a stone, like the sand...

'Please, sit down...' said Emanuel.

Solange fell into an armchair, slowly chewing her lips and every now and then sucking in the saliva running down her chin. She sat in the light, stock still, staring fixedly at the lampshade, without blinking, without being disturbed by the brightness, as if her eyes had been seized by the same apathy as her entire body, two mere pieces of glass encrusted in a stone face.

'You called… I came,' she said at last.

Emanuel sketched out a brief plan of attack for himself, stockpiled with arguments.

'I will need to speak as slowly and clearly as possible for her to understand me…' he thought to himself. 'She's completely demented… out of her mind with despair… I entirely understand,' he said out loud, an obvious tone of compassion in his voice. 'I understand, but all the same things couldn't have been otherwise. I know how painful our separation has been for you…'

He then lied, calmly:

'For you, and, as a matter of fact, also for me… I, too, am suffering, deep in my flesh, in my blood… you were a part of my own self.'

A flash of lightning suddenly streaked the room. Clouds were building up in the pitch-black sky outside, and thunder rolled, like a sudden and immense release of pent-up air. The heat was becoming harder and harder to bear; large beads of sweat covered Emanuel's forehead; the circular light of the lampshade sealed the room in a hermetic, suffocating space, like a glass bell submerged beneath the water.

'For me our separation was just as difficult… just as unbearable,' he continued. 'But I didn't want our love to become habit. Do you understand? I tried to find a way to save it from certain death by drowning in banality. I wanted something that was so pure, so extraordinary, to retain its uniqueness…'

'So pure, so extraordinary.' Solange repeated the words without comprehension. She waved her hand in front of her eyes as if to drive away an obsessive image, or perhaps a memory.

'And then,' Emanuel concluded, 'I only wanted to interrupt this love of ours. I never wanted to end it… I wanted to create a pause in it… a silence… in which it could become more focused and stronger…'

Everything that he said sounded in his head like a feeble explanation spoken by a stranger. He listened to himself talking with something like complaisance. The words themselves seemed to have atrophied in the heat. Where was this all taking place? What was certain was that night had fallen, with all its attendant revulsion and suffocation, into the water of a distorting mirror, and was now unfurling itself in the fragile and uncertain air on the other side of the glass…

Solange wrung her hands, twisting her fingers.

Suddenly she saw on the table the letter she had sent that morning. Following her gaze, Emanuel quickly snatched the paper and, in a dramatic gesture, unfolded it and tore it to pieces.

'What do you mean by these threats?' he said with sudden violence, throwing the torn pieces into an ashtray as if he was hurling them at Solange's face.

That was the final blow. It was, perhaps, the most atrocious, most brutal disappointment of the day. In profound humiliation she stared at the bits of paper in the ashtray, and even more than before, her face took on the submissive, meek air of a beaten animal.

'I repeat, our separation is only temporary,' Emanuel began again. 'And, even if it were for good…' he said, changing his mind, 'haven't we distilled all possible passion from our love? Everything that was unique and inimitable?'

'Yes, everything… everything…' repeated Solange, and it was clear that she did not know what she was saying. Then, her eyes barely open, she murmured:

'Can you hear…? The sea… The sea… it never stops surging…'

Weakly, she lifted a hand to her forehead.

Outside, in the night, the lighting was intensifying and the storm becoming more threatening, a tremendous struggle between the power of clouds that were ready to burst and the amorphous, annihilating heat that held them in their place. A few heavy drops rattled sharply on the roof, but a volley of wind burst upon the rain and drove it into the distance. It was very late. The cook might be snooping at the door. Emanuel was seized by impatience.

'All this stress… All this aggravation! You could have saved me the trouble!' he shouted furiously. 'Don't you realise that I am… an ill man? An invalid?'

At these words he fell to pieces: all the exhaustion, the sweat under his plaster, the evening's upheaval, made him suddenly lose control of himself. He burst into tears. Yes, Emanuel cried, shedding large, salt tears, and drank them in through the corner of his mouth… He covered his face with his hands, he hid under the blankets. He was redeemed: he cried, that was all, and he no longer wanted to know about anything around him. Solange could stay all night long or leave there and then. He heard her stand up and walk to his stretcher-bed. Then he felt the fall of a heavy body onto him, on top of the blankets.

'Forgive me… Emanuel… Forgive me…'

Solange was gasping and sobbing with despair. Ah, no! This he couldn't cope with! Him, weeping beneath the blankets, and her, above, hair disheveled, arms open in an attitude of penitence, like in an engraving… ah! no! A genuine urge to laugh came over him now. He wiped away his tears and spoke from under the covers.

'When are you leaving? You'll be caught in the rain…'

'This minute,' replied Solange through her sobs.

Emanuel uncovered his head.

Solange, purged by her tears, seemed to come to her senses. She did up her hair a little in front of the mirror, then made to leave.

'Forgive me, Emanuel… I forgot that you are an ill…'

'An invalid.' Emanuel finished her sentence.

She caught sight of the objects on the table, and wanted to take them with her.

'Please! Leave them here!' said Emanuel viciously.

It's better, he reasoned, that she knows she left me visible proof of madness. Tomorrow, in full daylight, it will torment her a little…

Solange left the room.

'Finally! Finally, alone…' said Emanuel to himself exultantly. He wiped his face and hands with a towel. He heard her footsteps outside, walking away, and then a thunderclap, sustained and impressive, like machine-gun fire. For a moment, he thought that lightning might strike Solange, and the idea, far from disturbing him, he found rather reviving.

With the tips of his fingers he managed to reach down a bottle of alcohol from a shelf. He poured it on his arms, he rubbed it on the back of his neck, on his face, on his throat, and the strong smell made him a little dizzy; he breathed the revivified air into his lungs until the sharpness of the alcohol burned his nose.

Exhausted by the heat, a little intoxicated from the alcohol fumes, he sat up, his head propped on his pillows, motionless, completely worn out, and thoroughly contented.

He lay like this for a long time, breathing slowly and rhythmically until he heard the rain beginning to fall outside, a good and gentle rain, a shower to soothe away the day's oppressive heat and terrible adventures.

20

T HE VERY NEXT morning Emanuel was due to go to the clinic
in order to be 'undressed' of his plaster.

The rain had cleansed the atmosphere and the events of the
previous night; on the table, in the fresh cold light of morning, the
shoe and the dead bird that Solange had brought seemed wholly
unreal and devoid of importance. He washed himself profusely,
allowing streaks of water to run under the cast (at other times he did
everything in his power to avoid this) in order to wallow miserably
in the sloshing moisture in which he lay, to torture himself for a
few more moments before discarding the corset.

The affair with Solange had ended cleanly and definitively; now
it was as if the cast alone remained as a last vestige of the horrible
adventure. I will take off all my memories of her along with it, he
told himself.

He was accompanied in the carriage by Irving, and it was as if this adolescent presence rejuvenated the very air itself. They went along streets entirely new, on a morning absolutely new, as generous and sonorous as a crystal goblet.

They drove straight into the courtyard of the clinic. Emanuel was expected, and the attendants quickly unloaded him and took him inside. The voluminous figure of Dr. Cériez appeared at once, entering the consulting room with a smile left over from a conversation next door. He leaned over Emanuel's stomach attentively and felt the area of the abscess with his fingers.

'Good… it's perfect,' the doctor muttered with satisfaction. 'We'll remove your cast today, and in a month or two you may be able to start walking…'

From a table he picked up an enormous pair of scissors like a garden tool, its points wrapped in protective gauze, and introducing it beneath Emanuel's white tunic, he began to cut the hard, thick shroud.

His face reddened with the intensity of effort. The nurse, pulling with all her might, detached one fragment after another, and tossed them in a bucket. For Emanuel it was as if his inner, private being was shedding its hermetic, oppressive shell. The carapace cracked at all its joints and the dry gauze from the plaster cast filled the room with a suffocating white dust.

Emanuel's exaltation grew with each piece that came off. Finally, the last fragment of the corset was torn away from his naked body.

But it was not his body of old. A revolting blanket of stinking, grey filth covered him almost all over, a thick layer of disgusting grime that fell from him in great crusts and filled him with revulsion.

The nurse brought a bottle of petroleum. Emanuel shut his eyes. 'Please give me back my body clean and intact, as it was when I entrusted it to you, before you put on the plaster cast,' he said.

Eva set to work, rubbing his skin with wet cotton swabs.

When he opened his eyes a little, Emanuel found that a territory of skin had come up small and pink from beneath the filth. As a child, on rainy days, he would wait with the same impatience for the asphalt to dry on the pavements so he could watch clear spots appearing… Slowly, the strip of cleanliness grew over his chest, then his thighs…

Ecstatically Emanuel touched the skin with his fingers. Its former tactility reawakened, like a calligraphy of tiny, precise trickles running and snaking below the surface. He wanted to leap off the stretcher-bed and take off at a run, anywhere, on the beach, naked, clean, luminous…

Eva helped him put on his shirt, then the rest of his clothes. They fluttered about him now like scarves; the shirt found no intimate point of contact with his body; it seemed to float in its entirety above his flesh, with its new-born, slightly sensitive skin.

In order to calm his elation (and indeed it felt as if his very body had begun to boil with contentment beneath his skin) he asked to be taken to the garden.

Now that it was summer, the patients no longer sat in the large area behind the sanatorium with its lawns and flowers. That was filled with tables and chairs for summer tourists who sprawled on deckchairs sipping lemonade, or spent the whole time turning gramophone handles.

A space was now reserved for the invalids, away from the sanatorium next to the stables, in a small cement courtyard surrounded by bushes like screens designed to hide them. This was where Emanuel was taken. The sun burned fiercely and the patients unashamedly discarded their blankets, displaying their legs and plaster bodies in broad daylight. In a corner he found Zed, as always with his pipe in his mouth, his legs stuck in their little plaster trunk, calmly, nonchalantly smoking with his usual gestures, as if the upper half of his body had nothing to do with the mutilated bits below it.

He also spotted the son of an Austrian with whom he had often talked in the hall. He had begun to walk and he now moved slowly through the courtyard, supporting himself on crutches. He wore a special cast, the one always used by patients beginning to walk, to get them used to holding their body erect for short periods of time.

The chest was entirely encased in a corset, which extended up to a round opening at the back of the neck, thus keeping the head rigid and unable to turn to the right or left.

The patient had to walk with his gaze fixed in front of him, like a blind man testing the ground, or the walking statue of some solemn-faced visionary.

'This is the fifth day I've been able to stand,' the little boy explained to Emanuel, looking at his watch, 'and I've got one more minute to go…'

Each day the convalescing patients tried to walk for one minute longer than on the previous. When they managed to stay on their feet for an entire half hour, all the supine patients envied them dreadfully; they were thought of as quite the healthiest, fittest people in the entire world.

'So what do you want to be when you grow up?' Emanuel asked, randomly.

'An aviator,' replied the boy proudly.

The corset reaching up to his chin, and the forward-frozen gaze, did give him something of the look of an airman; all that was missing was the leather headgear and goggles. Small details in a person's exterior appearance or dress can, in just this way, express their inner thoughts.

In a corner, dignified in her lace and an enormous velvet gown, enthroned on her carriage, the 'Marquise' was knitting with great attentiveness to her handiwork.

Further along, a tent of thin canvas covered part of the courtyard. The air filtering into this restricted space was clearer and more colourful, like in a glass cube, enclosing the patients in a fantastic display of crippled bodies like exhibits in a waxworks museum.

Emanuel edged his hand beneath his shirt and felt his ribs with secret satisfaction.

Suddenly someone came leaping towards him and shouting.

It was Katty, the redheaded Irish girl, whom he had not seen for a long time. She wore a simple red dress that draped her body like a sack; her breasts almost bared themselves with each heavy, panting breath.

Her skin was sunburnt all over. She had freshly scabbing sores on her arms and shoulders; her entire body was no more than a specimen of peeling flesh.

'Are you here with your carriage?' she asked. 'Will you take me with you for a drive?'

Then, wrapping her arms about his neck:

'Look how hot I am... I spent the entire day in the sun... I'm burning inside like a torch, and when I go in the sea, the water around me hisses, like a live coal dropped in a glass...'

Emanuel called for the attendant to load him in the carriage. Irving went off into town, and so, once the servant had gone, Emanuel was left alone in the carriage with Katty.

'This is a nice place you've got here...' said the girl, stretching out in the awning's shadow. 'It's like a little alcove...'

She began laughing with noisy snorts.

'And where are you planning to go this morning?' she asked.

Emanuel felt free and easy.

'Anywhere,' he replied, 'anywhere... this morning I'm in possession of a body I can do exactly what I like with... I found it again a moment ago, and I don't know what to do with it by myself...'

Katty laughed again in amusement.

'I know a really cool, shady place not far from Berck...' she said. 'What do you think? Shall we go for a drive there?'

They left the town, and for a while they sped in full sunshine along a lonely country road amidst rocky white fields like dry sea-beds. Katty took control of the horse.

She took a sudden turn behind a small group of houses and went over a railway crossing. They came into damp, verdant country so utterly unlike the barren fields they had coursed through until then that it seemed the tracks, gleaming on the railway bed, had severed the landscape, slicing it into two distinct zones of desert and vegetation. They struggled along a tunnel of bushes and foliage; the horse pushed aside branches on both sides with her head, making slow progress through the tall, wild grass.

It was a path nobody would have imagined was there, hidden among the dense branches. Eventually they came into a chamber of towering shadows. It was a great hall of trees and plants, with a carpet of short grass and walls of rustling willows. At one side a brook purled with the quiet plashing of a living, mysterious presence.

Emanuel breathed in deeply as if eagerly drinking a glass of very cold water after a tormenting thirst. He took off his shirt and lay topless, wrapped in pleasurable sheets of cool air.

Katty tied the horse to a tree stump.

'What are you doing? Have you gone mad?' she asked, pulling a face merrily when she saw him shirtless, and she hurled herself playfully down onto the grass, stretching out her limbs like a cat.

Now more than ever his supine position on the stretcher-bed, far away from the fresh cool grass, seemed intolerable to Emanuel; he wanted to roll on the ground too, he wanted to…

With a sudden movement he raised himself on his elbows and gripped one of the springs of the carriage's hood. Then, slowly, cautiously, he raised his leg and placed it on the wing of the carriage. He did not so much step down as fall onto the grass. Katty leapt to her feet with alarm when she saw him.

'Are you mad, absolutely mad!?' she babbled, slightly pale from the shock. 'You could catch your death of cold,' she cried, and rushed to the carriage, grabbing his coat to wrap him in.

As she slipped it on his back, her fingers touched his chest, and he shivered as if a shocking current had coursed through his flesh. How long had it been since he had felt the touch of another's hand? It was as if she had touched a new Emanuel, smooth, velvety, his new-made skin vibrant and hypersensitive. Rolling in the grass, he suddenly grasped her bare legs and embraced them in his arms, touching his forehead to them and kissing her coarse, rough knees.

'What are you doing? What are you doing?' cried Katty as she fell beside him into a passionate embrace.

'What are you doing?' she murmured again, and turned her head on the grass, her eyes shut, her breathing heavy as if in slumber, while he lifted off her dress, beneath which, on those summer days, she wore nothing else, not even a shirt.

He glued his lips to her red, sunburnt skin. She tried once more to struggle, but then lay motionless, pinned by his strength. Then he circled her in his arms and, with a sudden movement, rolled over onto her, his naked chest pressed to her burning bosom, in a thrash of wild, disordered movements, like a blaze of living, human flames.

21

CELINA CAME TO Villa Elseneur one afternoon, bringing bad news about Isa.

The illness had suddenly and inexplicably taken a turn for the worse. Isa suffered from an exotic disease which she had contracted in the Far East. Her entire right leg was now nothing but open sores and fistulas. They had carried out analyses and treatments for many years, but to no avail; her flesh continued to waste away and the only recourse was for Isa to lie flat on her trolley.

Many patients came to Berck ultimately requiring nothing except to lie down and to be among other invalids, to ease their protracted suffering.

'It's possible they will have to amputate her leg,' said Celina, trying to hold back her tears.

She patted her eyes with a handkerchief incessantly, but

was unable to stop weeping. She had, surely, been carrying this bitter, convulsive grief within her for years and now she had the opportunity to let it out.

'Does Isa know?' asked Emanuel.

'Oh, no! She doesn't suspect anything… Everyone around her is trying to hide the truth from her, as best we can… The doctor told her they might need to operate in order to clean the diseased area, so that she can start walking again… And she's happy… so happy… she thinks she's nearly cured…'

She wiped her eyes as the sobs continued to hiccough from deep within her chest.

'Please forgive me for making such a scene…'

She fell silent, staring at the floor and shaking her head slowly, as if to underscore an interior monologue.

She suddenly remembered something. 'I came to tell you on her behalf that she would like you to visit her… you haven't been for a while…'

Emanuel promised to come the next day.

'Oh, that's wonderful! Tomorrow her new dress will be ready,' said Celina. 'I feel so sorry for her… She really thinks she will be able to walk again and wants a new dress… "A light summer dress, with lots of flowers" is what she told me… Of course I wasn't going to argue with her so I had one made. It's a beautiful muslin dress… You'll see it. Please tell her how well it suits her…'

'What time should I come?'

'It's best if you come early, before four o'clock… as her fever starts afterwards and she becomes restless…'

* * *

Early next day Emanuel went into town in his carriage. He came across a little girl with a flower basket. She had a few small bouquets, completely colourless, made from the frail little plants growing on the dunes. He bought several bouquets and then went to a florist's and added some red carnations.

It was a singular bouquet now, an odd mix of lacklustre colour and vivid blooms. When Isa received it, she clutched it hard to her chest and then took a carnation and slipped it into her hair.

She was wearing her new dress and lay upon her carriage without any covers. The thin wisp of muslin did indeed become her. It reached below her knees; but while one leg was visible and dressed normally in a stocking and shoe, the other was entirely wrapped in thick gauze bandages.

She tucked the red flower behind her ear, and, examining the effect in a mirror, arranged her hair coquettishly.

The fever had painted her cheeks with two spots of red, like make-up. With a wave of her hand she tossed her hair aside, uncovering her forehead. She looked like a large doll placed on a bed; a doll with a broken leg, wrapped in white rags by a little girl playing doctor.

The blinds were drawn and the light filtered into the room with difficulty, accompanied by the low hum of the warm, quiet afternoon.

The same vague, festering smell hung round the room, but more stale, more penetrating perhaps than before. Celina brought two large glasses of orangeade.

While they sipped it an attendant came in to announce that someone was waiting outside. 'He's here again,' said Celina in annoyance. 'Please, don't let him in today…' she said to Isa, 'I implore you.'

But Isa ignored her.

'Let him come in… tell him to come in… today, I'm not afraid… because today, Emanuel is here…'

She directed her gaze towards him.

'How grateful I would be if you could help me escape from this obsession! But it's impossible… He says he can heal me with the aid of astral bodies… Do you know what that is? Mysterious powers… communication with the spirits…'

She spoke incoherently, and, it seemed, a little fearfully.

A little man came in, walking with a contorted limp. His round, swollen shoulder appeared first, followed by his thrust-out chest. His face was hideous, partially ravaged by pockmarks, with eyes like orbs popping out of their sockets. He wore an ancient heavy overcoat with a velvet collar, but did not seem uncomfortable in the day's heat.

'I bring you good news,' he told Isa, manifestly ignoring Emanuel's presence, and cracking his fingers quietly. 'Last night, I entered into communication with a great spirit who seems to be favourable to you.'

His voice had a hoarse quality, like a sort of weak rattling.

Emanuel suddenly spotted something black on the little man's neck and, looking at it more closely, he realised that it was a bedbug. He was overcome by an immediate wave of disgust mixed with inexpressible pity.

Isa, however, gazed transfigured at the man with intense emotion, while her hands began to shake slightly. The tiny man had clearly managed to control and intimidate her.

'I bring you a sign from the spirit...' the little man went on, pulling a small package wrapped in newspaper from his waistcoat pocket. 'It is a fragment of astral rock. I beg you to take very good care of it...'

Isa took it and burrowed it deep among her pillows. Her teeth began to chatter with fear.

'I am sorry that I cannot stay long today...' added the tiny man. 'This evening, at nine twenty-five, you must think intently about the spirit...' he instructed Isa, from the doorway.

At last he was gone. Celina escorted him out and remained in the corridor speaking to him for a few moments.

'What an impostor! What a vile impostor...' Emanuel burst out after the door had closed. 'Celina is right: you must get rid of him...'

Isa looked at him in fear.

'I'm scared... Emanuel... he could avenge himself... do something horrible.'

At that moment, Celina walked in, rummaged through her purse, and immediately left again.

'I bet he asked you for money,' said Emanuel when she returned.

'Exactly. He asked me to lend him five francs.'

'May I see the astral body without its wrapping paper?' Emanuel asked.

Isa gave it to him. He opened the small bundle and examined its contents carefully. Then he brought it up to his nose:

'It's just a piece of cheese,' he said. 'Celina, look at it yourself.'

The nurse sniffed it and made a grimace of disgust. Isa wrenched the package from her hand and hid it beneath her head.

Emanuel was beside himself with fury.

'Why does he come to heal you rather than healing himself first, if he really is in communication with the great spirits? Why? Why does he walk so crookedly?'

He realised that he would not convince her this way.

There was only one route to take. Emanuel immediately composed himself and addressed Isa in a solicitous tone of voice:

'Perhaps… What do I know? Perhaps it's possible that this astral body really does have magical qualities… I'd like to try it, myself… Won't you lend it to me for a few days, to put it under my body? Who knows, after all…?'

Isa handed him the little packet with an air of great trust, and became more animated:

'You're not sure, are you…? This is what torments me too, this "perhaps"… Perhaps it's possible that…'

The red stains in her cheeks flared and fine pearls of sweat covered her temples. The fever had obviously reached its greatest pitch.

She added, as if confessing:

'As a matter of fact, I've been feeling much better the last few days… I have a fever… that's all… But what does that matter, so long as I am feeling better…?'

Celina left the room.

'I'll tell you a secret, Emanuel… my greatest secret. Yesterday and today I won a great number of days from Celina at cards… We played this morning…'

Emanuel was mystified.

'I will explain,' she continued. 'But you must not tell. Please, I implore you, you must not tell anyone… Every day I play cards with Celina. We've agreed we're not playing for stakes, but in my mind I play for days… days of my life… Each point I win from her means an extra day added to my life… but taken from hers. You understand?'

She began laughing apprehensively, in unnerving jolts, as if she could not entirely control her movements.

'This very morning I won another three hundred and fourteen days from her… What do you think? That's almost a year… And of course, she suspects nothing… but that's why she's becoming weaker, while I'm looking better and better…'

She had completely lost her composure. Spreading her fingers, she tousled her hair and stroked her forehead.

'I am waiting for the day when I have won all the days of my life… and she suddenly, sitting next to me, collapses exhausted and dies… Like one of those dolls that you fill up with air, that slowly deflates when you open the valve… yes… yes… I will win.'

She was quiet for a moment, then suddenly became extremely agitated:

'Do you know why I will win? This is the real secret… Do you hear me? Do you know why?'

She was nearly choking with excitement.

'Because…' she burst out. 'Because I cheat.'

She was on fire now, her cheeks burning, her hands restless.

'When I am well… I'm going to be a dancer… I shall tell you everything today, Emanuel… I'm going to dance naked with you…'

She shuddered suddenly at what she was saying, and slapped herself on the cheek.

'What am I saying? Have I gone insane?'

Emanuel would have liked to leave the room in a hurry, as every second was becoming more painful.

'You understand me, Emanuel… We'll be the greatest dancers in the world. And we'll dance to the music of Bach… We'll be the first people ever to dance to Bach… Do you understand? Do you understand? We will amaze the audience to the depths of their guts… of their guts… guts full of sh—… What am I saying? What am I saying?'

She began yelling:

'Hey, I'm not ashamed! I say it loud and clear, they have guts full of shit…! Shit…!'

Celina burst in the room, alarmed.

'Oh! There goes the fever again…' With calm and gentle movements she approached the bed and began rubbing Isa's temples to try to quieten her.

'Each time that little man comes, the same thing happens… She starts to get agitated and delirious.'

Isa fell back into her pillows, exhausted, while her lips continued to mutter something unintelligible.

They rang for an attendant, who wheeled Emanuel out of the room.

Celina hurried out after him into the corridor.

'She sent me… to tell you… to forgive her… she insisted that you forgive her.'

'For what? What has she done?' replied Emanuel sadly…

'She needs to forgive me. And us all... she's the one who must forgive us...'

A dried-up unhappiness weighed down on him, like a tearless sobbing from the depths of his chest, a grim afternoon melancholy.

Outside, in a back street, he took the astral body from his pocket and flung it into a sewer.

22

E MANUEL RECEIVED A LETTER.

Paris, September 7, 19—

My Dear Emanuel,

  Here I am again at last in Paris, after an absence of eight years. I escaped the sanatorium quietly and without saying goodbye to anyone. My parents came in a car and in half an hour I was packed, tied up with string and thrown in the back of the automobile. It's a superb 'roadster', the latest model with the latest improvements and an aerodynamic design, so aerodynamic that you have to sit crouched inside with your knees in your mouth like a prisoner in a cell. As far as comfort goes, I am convinced there is nothing so admirable as an invalid's stretcher-bed: you lie on it like a king while you are wheeled about by attendant as taciturn and solemn as an English lord.

What puzzled me first (in the most absurd way) about Paris was that I didn't see one single patient in a carriage anywhere. One day I did spot an invalid in his automatic carriage on a street corner and I wanted to rush over and kiss and hug him like a brother. But you know that in life it is precisely the gestures that make most sense that are forbidden.

I stared after him for a long time, this strange alluring mixture, half man, half bicycle.

Perhaps the legend of the Minotaur needs to be brought up to date.

I spend the entire day walking the streets and each footstep on the pavement re-echoes in my brain, clear, strong and independent as the blow of a hammer. I can't stretch out in a taxi except on my side and anyway I prefer to get used to walking.

Something odd happened to me yesterday: I read an advertisement on a house gate; they were looking for a 'technical' draughtsman. I know how to draw a little; the door was open and I couldn't not go in, could I? I had to climb up to the fifth floor. First I went up a sumptuous flight of stairs, with plush carpet and ornamental brass banisters. That was the staircase to the first floor. Then, the more I climbed, the more the stairs diminished in elegance and solidity, until I reached the last floor where I was forced to grope in near darkness to be able to make out a narrow wooden stairway, each step groaning with rottenness.

The advertisement from the gate was there as well, but nowhere was there a bell to be seen. I saw a half-open door and knocked, then waited. I stood there for a few minutes in the absolute silence of that strange house, leaning on the landing balustrade and staring out through the garret window over the city's roofs.

I think I waited for about ten minutes before knocking on the door once again, louder this time. Then, with the sudden impulse you get in the face of something forbidden, I opened the door. I found myself in a kind of workshop with large dusty windows, not wiped clean for months, I suppose. In the middle was an enormous table strewn with drawings and rolls of blue paper.

I waited a while longer, then rapped on the table with a set square. The knocks echoed and disappeared in the deserted house. There was another door, open, in front of me, and now of course I had to go on until I came across someone.

I went through without knocking. It was a room with a lot of things in it, piled up rather at random. In one corner, a large lamp on a stand with a shade of pink silk… a dignified old thing, next to a bed with lots of little columns and spirals. I cleared my throat, I made some noise, I sat on a stool, and still no one came. Was the house actually abandoned?

Eventually I discovered a door that connected with the rest of the apartment. It was covered with wallpaper and nearly invisible… It led to a kind of kitchen with shabby furniture. On a bowl on the table was a leftover salad. You can't imagine, Emanuel, how strange and abandoned an empty room can be, in which you discover the traces of people who lived there… Horrific impression of desolation and loneliness! I realised then that perhaps the objects and décor among which people spend their most familiar, most essential hours, do not in fact belong to anyone… People pass through them, that's all, the same way I passed through that unknown house, insensible of, and unconnected to, those piles of domestic intimacy that lay scattered around me.

I left feeling unbearably sad, but not without committing a last, completely absurd gesture, which alone could save me from the state of incomprehension in which I was floating. In the room furnished like a small parlour, there was an enormous gold-framed picture hanging on the wall, showing an officer leaning on his sword. Well, I paused before him, I stood to attention and gave him a quick, energetic, military salute. Do you understand? It was the stupidest gesture I could perform then and there. It was my supreme tribute to this mysterious room and the anonymous officer who alone, in the awful solitude of that house, still had a solid reason for existing and leaning on a sword. Unknown photograph, I salute you!

I leave to the end some really sensational news about Tonio. You may know that I am good friends with his brother. I often go to their home. One day last week I was there for tea. The thing I want to tell you about happened then.

Tonio had been interned for some time in a clinic near Paris in order to undertake a treatment to calm him down. Everything seemed to work out splendidly and soon he returned home, completely restored. At least that's what we all thought… The thing is, I found him more desperate, in more of a decline, and drunker than ever. As yet I still haven't breathed a word to his brother about what I've seen, and I don't know that I will: I'd rather try to make Tonio understand, though that will be difficult…

But to come back to what happened: a large number of people, many of them unknown to me, showed up at the aforementioned tea-party. Suddenly the door opened and a young engineer I know came in accompanied by a tall blonde woman wrapped in white ermine... Well, I was in shock; my jaw hung open while the teacup in my hand shook with emotion... The woman who had come in looked astoundingly like Madame Wandeska, so much so that if I didn't know that she had left the sanatorium limping I could have believed that it was her and would have gone up to her and started speaking like an old acquaintance ...

I looked round for Tonio, and found him in a corner of the room, pale, transfigured, his eyes fixed on the extraordinary, hallucinatory apparition... Everything, from the clothes, the white ermine, and the quick movements, to the gentle bell-like laughter: everything contributed to the illusion of a Madame Wandeska restored to our sight and frighteningly present...

Tonio sidled up to me, muttered a few words and quickly left for his room. I followed him there.

'Did you see?' he murmured.

'Indeed. Extraordinary...'

'Please forgive me...' he went on. 'I have a little something I have to take care of which won't allow any delay... and which I will actually attend to in your presence. Please forgive me, and try to understand...'

He walked to a wardrobe, took out a little box with a metal top, and placed it on the table. It contained a few different instruments; he took out a syringe. He selected a needle, which he held in the flame of a match. Then, without hurrying, with slow and certain movements, like a doctor who knows what he's doing, he filled the syringe with the contents of a vial, rolled up his sleeve and stabbed the needle deep into his skin...

'Have you been doing this long?' I asked him, dismayed.

'A nurse taught me how to do this at the clinic where I went for a "rest",' he said. 'It's stronger and more effective than, for instance, alcohol...'

I said nothing, shocked and lacking the courage to lecture him. I understand him, and perhaps he's right. Who knows, maybe one day it will be me... But no... definitely not... There are surer, more conclusive and quicker ways than this.

I won't go on now because I am terribly tired and I put aside even the pleasure of writing to you when I had a chance to sink into my dreams.

   With love,

   Ernest, who wishes you, if you want it, to get well quickly.

23

A FEW WEEKS had passed since Emanuel had been to see Isa. Autumn had returned to Berck with its foggy mornings and constant drizzle, leaving the rooms dim in the feeble light of an infinite melancholy.

Emanuel was always going to have to move back to the sanatorium at some point, as Mrs Tils would be leaving Villa Elseneur for the winter.

The return was dull and depressing. Emanuel came back to an empty, desolate sanatorium. Quitonce was dead, Tonio, Ernest and Roger Torn had left, and now Isa was undergoing an operation. Emanuel would stay in his room all day long, staring into space through the damp, cold windows... He now understood better, and more profoundly, what Ernest had once said to him:

'There are moments when you are "less than yourself" and less than everything. Less than whatever object you're looking at, less than a chair, than a table, less than a piece of wood. You are the bottom rung of things, at the lowest level of existence, beneath your own life and beneath what goes on around you… You are a form more ephemeral, more threadbare than that of the immutable base material of existence. You then need to expend immense effort just to understand the simple inertia of rocks, and you lie annihilated, reduced to being "less than yourself", in the impossibility of making that effort.'

Mrs Tils came to bid him farewell. It was a time of separations, departures and regrets. Zed called on him from time to time. His visits calmed Emanuel; for him, all this restlessness could be resolved with a simple, quiet smoke of his pipe.

In the garden, summer had ended; its greenery was suffering from a secret, internal disease, but one that was nonetheless not yet fatal. The leaves curled slightly like the hand of a dying man, clenching his fingers a little in a spasm of pain without otherwise moving. It was the phase of autumn when decay reigns supreme, a season of endings, when the geraniums scatter their bitter perfume more strongly and the dahlias fold their petals like miniature fireworks slowly snuffing out.

Celina paced the corridors anxiously. Emanuel encountered her a few times, but he didn't dare speak to her, and she seemed not to see anything in front of her.

She appeared in his room one evening, however, when Emanuel was lying with the light out, asleep. She tried to speak but began to whimper gently.

'Finally, a place where I can cry…' she said.

She tucked her head into her arm, resting on the chair, and would have looked as if she had dozed off had she not been shaken now and then with sobs.

'So how is Isa?' asked Emanuel.

'Isa is not well at all... She's much worse now, since the operation, worse than before... It gushes out of her like a fountain... It's horrible, especially when I have to bandage her in the morning. She would scream before, but now she can't even scream any more... Where her leg was cut from the thigh there is a wound you could fit a child's head in... gaping, ragged flesh... horrible, horrible...'

She spoke with a tremor in her voice and seemed obsessed by horrifying images.

'I wanted to keep the leg but they wouldn't let me. The whole length of the operation I stood by the door, lying in wait... You see, I wanted to get the leg and preserve it in alcohol... I'd got this idea into my head...'

'And they didn't give it to you?' asked Emanuel.

'Certainly not... Anyway, it's better that way... When Eva came out with it from the operation room, honestly I thought she had a bouquet of flowers in her hands. That's what the leg looked like, wrapped in cotton and gauze, all bloody... Like a magnificent bouquet of roses... oh, how insane of me...! When I realized it was Isa's leg, I ran as fast as I could after Eva. She was taking it to the basement, to burn it in the oven. What do you think of that? To burn it, to throw it in the fire... I felt I was losing my wits... it's as if I can see it burning now... I can't get it out of my mind!... I can see it catching fire and burning in the flames… and, the most horrible thing, when the fire reaches the sole of the foot, the toes suddenly spread out, just like they do when I cut her nails…'

She spoke slowly now, as if trying to free herself of the terrible burden.

'She's in a constant state of delirium… I barely understand what she's saying… She keeps insisting she wants to play cards with me…'

Emanuel remembered what Isa had said to him that day.

'Please play cards with her,' he told her. 'Let her win as much as you can…'

A few days passed quietly. Isa slept most of the time. It was a beneficial sleep, the doctor insisted.

Emanuel rode to the beach in his carriage. He found the sanatorium suffocating and preferred to pass long hours in the rain, with the carriage top up, by the shore of the ocean, rather than in his melancholy, white room. Solange accompanied him once again, but as a good friend now, calm and taciturn, with obliging, discreet gestures, speaking to him in whispers, as if they were both wary of awakening some bitter and painful thing that was waiting to erupt inside them…

One day on the beach they met some children, carrying something they had spotted on the sand in a noisy convoy. It was a dead jellyfish, a great chunk of gelatinous, transparent flesh, with an acrid reek of fish and iodine. Solange shuddered in horror. Emanuel took the creature in his hand; its mucous mass stuck strangely to his skin. The soft dank chill seeped through him into his brain. He closed his eyes, a little feverish.

'To me, my own soul feels like this inert, disgusting piece of life,' he muttered. 'Berck is full of this kind of enlightening apparition… What a stink of putrefaction it exhales…'

And Emanuel recalled his last visit to Isa's room and the festering stench permeating it… He gave the jellyfish back and decided to return to the sanatorium. The rotting sea-corpse had made the deepest impression on him, like a sort of omen, real and manifest in a lump of wet, cold flesh.

Isa was much worse. She was connected to an oxygen tank and being fed intravenously. The apparition of the jellyfish had indeed been mysteriously prophetic.

Then, one evening, Isa died.

Celina came straight to Emanuel's room. She had brought some of the dead woman's things to leave in his care.

'She asked me to give them to her father but I am afraid to keep them there… they could get lost in all the coming and going…'

She no longer wept, and was almost calm.

'She is so white and beautiful and peaceful in her bed. I think that she has finally found some peace. It's as if she's sleeping in a perfect state of grace…'

Emanuel tossed and turned all night in bitter, hallucinatory dreams. It was as if the room itself was filled with a putrid, enfeebling breath, like the pulp of a jellyfish…

…And despite this, outside the sun was shining, a wondrous white and brilliant sun in a cloudless summer sky. Emanuel found himself at the center of a sports arena. All the benches, though, were empty. He was alone, absolutely alone, on an asphalt racetrack. In full sunshine. And all of a sudden, with a leap, Zed appeared. He was clothed in his running gear, his red shirt emblazoned with an enormous initial.

'You see…? I'm cured, I've begun walking,' he said.

Emanuel took a closer look at him and noticed his curious legs. When had they been severed? Below his knees, only the calves remained; his feet had been removed, and in the place where the legs had been cut, circular pieces of metal had been fixed, like the lids of two tin cans. When he bounced upon the asphalt he made an unbearable metallic sound… Clack!… Clack!… Clack! …

And Zed went off, as if on stilts. It was so hot that the sun melted the asphalt. Slowly the stadium turned to pitch, warm and yielding… The further Zed went, the deeper he sank into asphalt… up to his knees… to his thighs… then his head… On the spot where he sank out of sight, there remained on the surface of the track a thin, transparent tissue of pink skin, like a water blister on a burning leg…

That morning Emanuel was due to be taken to have his consultation with Dr Cériez. He found his patient pale and changed.

'What's wrong with you?' asked the doctor. 'Tell me everything, please… your well-being is as important to me as the state of your vertebrae…'

Emanuel's eyes were filled with tears.

'I can't stay on at Berck… it's more than I can handle… the sadness of this town is killing me… all the world's melancholy has collected here…'

The doctor remained quiet for a while, thinking intently.

'What if you left? Take a short break in Switzerland, say, for a few months. I think that a change of climate would do you good…'

'I've been thinking about it for a while myself,' said Emanuel. 'But how can I go anywhere lying on a stretcher-bed?'

'That's the easiest thing in the world,' smiled the doctor. 'There is a night express going directly from Boulogne to Geneva… you take the little evening train from Berck to where it joins the main line, and there you board a special compartment on the express… and the next day you get off at your destination. You might be able to get a nurse to accompany you… there are Swiss nurses in Paris who accompany patients, and they're always shuttling between Paris and Geneva… I could find out for you.'

Emanuel decided to leave in a week.

24

D EPARTURE DAY, a day of final confrontations.

Emanuel hired a carriage in order to take one more look at all the old places.

First to the dunes, to Villa Elseneur. It was an autumn day, warm and sunny, just as it had been a year before when he had arrived in Berck.

He bade farewell to the innkeeper and his wife and the few sailors... They drank absinthe together, and the men wished Emanuel a quick recovery. Under the midday sun, in the desolation of the dunes, the words sounded strange. Somewhere this afternoon, a girl lay buried under the earth, a pale girl with a dark fringe who had once coquettishly put a red carnation behind her ear. And a young man, grown old too quickly, who had once shown him pornographic photographs. In what reality did the dunes still exist, and the warm light of the sun, and Emanuel himself, lying in a carriage… with hands that moved… with eyes that saw… with the clear hum of the afternoon singing in his head? The world's desolation had become infinite.

He went to where Celina lived on the edge of town, with her sister and brother-in-law, a fisherman, in a humble cottage so low he could touch the eaves of the roof with his hand.

In the courtyard fishing nets dried in the sun. Celina emerged through the low door, all hunched up as if crawling out of a lair. The passage of a few days had wrinkled her face like a dried, rotten piece of fruit.

They spoke about Isa, recalling her with memories so pure and so calm that their grief became a luminous thing, mysterious and still in the spotless silence of afternoon; and also a sunrise, a solemn lighting up of their hearts.

'I felt sorry that I had to bury her without her leg,' she said. 'It was too sad… too distressing. Still, I tried to hide the horror of that image and I put a garland of flowers in the coffin in place of the leg they cut off… lilies and tuberoses… her favourite flowers…'

Emanuel wandered for a while longer on the town's narrow, sad streets. Then he returned to the clinic to make his final preparations for departure. He was escorted to the train by two attendants who helped him into the compartment, and a Swiss nurse who had come from Paris to accompany him onwards.

In the evening, Dr Cériez, too, came to see him off on the platform.

Emanuel had just settled into the little branch-line train when Solange burst into the carriage, flustered at having nearly missed him.

She came alongside him, so out of breath that she scarcely had the strength to mutter a few words.

'Please forget, Emanuel,' she said. 'Forget everything… especially that horrible night… Forget this town… forget its agonies…'

She leaned over him, kissed his forehead, and slipped from the compartment quickly, to stop herself from bursting into tears.

The little train started to move slowly, rattling away on the rails.

The nurse began to knit under the bulb's weak light.

Emanuel lay motionless for some moments, then lifted himself on his elbows and looked out of the window.

In the distance the town, like a sinking ship, was disappearing in the darkness.

THE END